Ramu Prasad's Angel

Ramu Prasad's Angel

Tayenjam Bijoykumar Singh

PARTRIDGE
A Penguin Random House Company

Some of the stories in this collection have appeared elsewhere: 'Eche-Nungshirei' and 'Loneliness' in *Chandrabhaga* (15/2007 and 8/2003), 'The Flight' in *Melange* (31 July, 2005), 'Fifty Years', 'Recharge Card' and 'Your Story' in *NEWFRONTIERS* (Vol. I No.2, 1999, Vol. VI No.1, 2007 and Vol. VII No.1, 2009) and 'Mauled Cub' in *The Oxford Anthology of Writings from North-East India; Fiction* (First published 2011).

To order additional copies of this book, contact
Partridge India
000 800 10062 62
www.partridgepublishing.com/india
orders.india@partridgepublishing.com

CONTENTS

For my parents
who taught me
'Humanity is the best religion.'

1

Eche-Nungshirei

It is this story of an incident hovering inside my head that has been troubling me for so many years—it has left a deep imprint in my life. On several occasions I have tried to tell it to my friends to lessen the burden of keeping it a secret. But something at the back of my head always stops me short, "No, no, don't tell the story. It may put an indelible blot in Eche-Nungshirei's spotless character and spoil her life."

I want to wipe the story off my memory but a young woman, a patient of mine, has revived it anew like new shoots sprouting from the dormant buds of a tree at the outset of the spring. A rare case, someone in my profession as a neurologist would have called it an interesting case but I would rather not do so for her life is at stake. She has indications of dystonia and myoclonus. Examination of her eye movements and other symptoms are confirming it. During the last one year, she has not shown any improvement. Her intellectual, physical and emotional capabilities are diminishing. Her health is also gradually deteriorating. She has just turned thirty-one but it seems her life is slipping away, slowly but steadily. My diagnosis can be wrong. It's exactly what I wish to happen. If I could I would gladly give her life back to her.

I have a strong feeling that the story in my head is somehow connected with her life. Her parents are not aware of it. Emotion stirs in my little heart, the existence of which I have forgotten long ago. "O God! How I wish to save her!"

I had spent a part my of childhood days at a village where my father worked as a teacher of the only government school there, a very prestigious job in those days. He commanded respect of one and all; some of it had even been rubbed off to me as well, being the only son of *Ojha* as referred to a teacher with respect. Though the school was a government school, the teachers were not provided accommodation. But the villagers provided a house with a spacious compound for us to stay as a gesture of goodwill and respect to my father. It is a pity that nowadays no one respects a teacher of a government school.

How I cherish the bygone days! No hurrying and scurrying around, life was quite peaceful. Away from the maddening crowd of towns and cities, my life in the village was closely associated with nature. Bamboo groves, open meadows, rice fields, canals and ponds were our playfields. Whenever I got a chance, I used to ride in bullock-carts. The slow and steady rhythmic movement and the low continuous squeaky noise the wheels made never failed to exhilarate me. Jingling of the bells on some of the bullocks' necks provided soft music on such rides.

In the village, there was no homestead without a pond and bamboo groves at the back. Almost every family owned a pair of bullocks and a bullock-cart. The villagers depended heavily on bullocks for their survival and economy. Bullocks were used to pull carts for transportation and to plough rice fields, their major source of income. Naturally, bullocks were cared with love and treated as members of the family.

Growing rice was the main occupation of the villagers. They also grew vegetables to meet their requirement and sell off the excess. Some families had taken up pisciculture to supplement their income. After harvesting rice, straw was not discarded but neatly tied in bundles and stacked around bamboo poles erected in their compounds. Straw was used to thatch houses and feed cattle. It was cut into small pieces and mixed with mud to plaster the walls of their wattle and daub houses. Sometimes, it was used instead of wood as fuel for cooking.

I used to roam around everywhere with my friends and play wherever we liked. No one would say a thing until and unless we touched the straw-stacks. Nevertheless when elders were not around, we played with straw—rolling on it, climbing to the top of the stacks and come sliding down. Sometimes, the straw bundles came down tumbling while playing. We immediately put the bundles back in place. We were careful not to scatter straw around.

Then, there was the woods a little way off from the village, a place revered to the villagers, zealously protected and preserved by them—a sacred place where *Umang Lai*, a sylvan deity, the deity of the village, presided. Many big trees with vines and creepers twisting around the trunks grew there. Most prominent among the trees was a huge banyan tree. Its branches supported by prop roots spread over a wide area. The prop roots had grown very thick and looked actually like trunks, giving the impression of a number of trees growing with the branches joined together. People said, "One night, it started turning into an elephant but could not complete the transformation as day broke too soon."

In the centre of the woods, there was a clearing where a small temple dedicated to *Umang Lai* stood. Every year *Lai Haraoba*, meaning merrymaking or pleasing of deity, a festival, was celebrated with much enthusiasm in the summer. During the festival, people from far and wide came to witness and participate in folk dance, race, wrestling bouts and *kangjei*, a traditional game of hockey played with bamboo sticks.

The woods was the only place we avoided while playing. The sight of the banyan tree was so frightening that it sent shivers down the spine and gave us the creeps. Elders of the village also warned us, "Don't enter the woods. Many spirits, ready to pounce on the unlucky ones, reside there." Only during *Lai Haraoba* when people thronged to the temple, we entered the woods without any inhibition.

There were many stories circulating about the woods. Ta-Tomchou's father, a foolhardy man, did not heed to the warnings of the elders. One day, he entered the woods at noon to relieve himself. A spirit entered his body. He soon started losing his physical strength and intellectual capabilities. Before long he, an athletic man, was reduced to a mere weakling. He could no longer walk without support. He also had frequent seizures. Many shamans and exorcists were summoned and consulted but no amount of exorcism could drive away the spirit that had possessed him. He did not live to see his thirty-fifth birthday. At that time Ta-Tomchou was not more than five. It was also said that his grandfather died in the same manner under similar circumstances. Behind their back people murmured, "*Umang Lai* has cast a spell on the family for defiling Her abode."

When I came to know Ta-Tomchou, he had already crossed his teens. Elders called him Tomchou but I used to call him Ta-Tomchou or big-brother-Tomchou like other children did. He lived with his widowed mother in a small house near the main road where they opened a tea stall and ran a grocery shop. Both the mother and son were engaged in running their business. Their place was not very far from our house. I often went there on errand to get what my mother wanted. In the evening, most of the girls and boys in the village would flock at their tea stall. In a way it served as a 'Lovers' Den'.

Ta-Tomchou was well built and handsome, the heart-throb of many a girl in the village. I often saw the girls nudging him to help them in petty matters just to attract his attention. He would silently do whatever he was asked to do like an obedient child without even lifting his eyes to glance at them. But, I had a feeling that he had a liking for Eche-Nungshirei who lived next to our house. To the elders she was Nungshirei or Nungshi only but to me she was Eche-Nungshirei, *Eche* meaning 'elder sister'.

She was the only child of her parents, who were said to be rich by the village's standard. In the village, it was considered a good fortune to have many children, at least one male child to continue the lineage. But, whenever the subject of having a son was brought up by the elders her father would say, "Son or daughter, I see no difference. To me, Nungshirei is both a son and a daughter." Another story also circulated about Eche-Nungshirei. Her parents considered her to be a gift of *Umang Lai*. Even after the lapse of seven years of their marriage, her parents were issueless. Desperate for a child, they visited many temples, took the advice of elders, consulted shamans and took a number of herbal medicines and concoctions but it was of no use. When they had almost given up their hope, on the advice of a priestess they ardently prayed to *Umang Lai* for a child of their own during *Lai Haraoba*. Eche-Nungshirei, a miracle child, was born a year later.

Their homestead must be not less than two acres in area. Their house facing to the east was a big one with corrugated iron sheet roof, a symbol of affluence in those days. Their courtyard in front of the house was always spick and span. They had a spacious *mamang-sangoi*, an outhouse on the eastern side of the courtyard where sixty to sixty-five persons could sit comfortably at a time and a smaller *makha-sangoi*, another outhouse on the southern side. On the northern side of the courtyard, there was a shed where they kept a pair of bullocks. They used their *makha-sangoi* for keeping their bullock-cart and a big wooden pestle for pounding rice. Their *mamang-sangoi* served as the meeting place of the village. Beyond it there was a pond. In the space between the *mamang-sangoi* and the pond, gardenia and rose bushes grew in two neat rows. Near the pond, on the northern side, a mango tree grew. Next to the mango tree, they stacked straw. Their straw-stack was considerably high, which showed the size of the rice field they owned. On the southern side of the pond, there was a big garden where they grew all sorts of vegetables throughout the year. A bamboo grove and a wide ditch beyond it, which also served as a drain, separated their compound from ours. From our backyard, we could see the pond and their garden. But their courtyard and house were hidden from view by their *mamang-sangoi*. I often saw Eche-Nungshirei either fetching water from the pond or plucking flowers from the gardenia and rose bushes.

Eche-Nungshirei treated Ta-Tomchou as her big brother. Like a sister, she would often crack jokes and sing songs calling him funny names to tease him. Her voice was really sweet. She had a natural talent for singing. With proper training, she could easily have become a good professional singer. Remembering the way she used to sing, I still feel sorry for her to have wasted her rare inborn gift. Looking at the way she fooled around with Ta-Tomchou, everyone in the village said, "In their earlier births, they were brother and sister."

While I was studying in class V, one day I heard that Eche-Nungshirei had been betrothed to someone from a far off place and her marriage was fixed on an auspicious day in *Phairel*, a month according to Manipuri calendar falling in January-February. Her aunt had arranged the match. A sudden change came over her. She was no longer her usual jolly self. She stopped going around in the company of her friends and mixing with Ta-Tomchou as in the earlier days.

One fine Monday morning, I came out to play with my friends but no one was around. I still remember that day very vividly. Being *Phairel Panchami* or the fifth day of *Phairel*, it was holiday for us. It was the day we celebrated *Swaraswati Puja* a festival dedicated to *Swaraswati,* the Hindu goddess of learning. Unlike other schools in towns and cities, we performed only the ceremonial rite of *Swaraswati Puja* on *Phairel Panchami* but the other activities of students associated with it were postponed till the next day.

My father, being a teacher, was busy in making arrangements for the ceremonial rite in school. My mother also had accompanied him to help, an opportunity she would never miss. They wanted me to come along but I stayed behind feigning to have a mild headache. They left after warning me to stay inside the house. The moment they left the house, I came out running and went to my friends' houses. But, to my utter dismay, I found their houses locked.

Phairel Panchami is a very important occasion for the villagers. On this day, the whole of the families except the old and infirm go to rice fields early in the morning for the ceremonial first ploughing of the year. But women and children do not set their feet in the rice fields.

It is considered a bad omen. Instead, they hang around in sheds or comfortable places near the rice fields where the men are working to wait on them and give food and water when they are tired.

All my friends had followed their parents to their rice fields. Disheartened, I went alone to the bamboo grove at the back of our house where we had cleared a patch for hiding. It served as our camp while playing our 'war' game. When I reached the clearing, the ground was still wet with dew. I went in the house and brought a rug-sack. I laid it on the ground and sat on it, contemplating on the many games we used to play there.

After a while, I heard someone singing quite far away in the neighbour's compound. Even though it was barely audible, I could still recognize the sweet voice. Through the thick mesh of bamboo branches, I saw Eche-Nungshirei with a melodious song on her lips, holding a *sanabun*, a traditional long-necked brass pot, in her right hand, going towards the pond. She must have come to fetch water. When she reached the straw-stack near the pond, someone suddenly accosted her. I could not see the other person's face as his back was turned to me. He was wearing a chequered *khudei*, traditional male attire, a loincloth worn like dhoti but reaching to the knees and a sleeveless white shirt. The person's dress could not provide any clue to his identity as everyone in the village wore similar dress. The distance between them and me also was another factor leading to my failure to recognize him. She did not show any surprise. She stopped singing and they started talking. It meant, the person was known to her. But my inquisitiveness made me watch them without batting an eye. "Is he her lover?" But, as far as my knowledge about her was concerned, she did not have any lover. If she had one, it would have been known to everyone in the village. In the close-knit society of the village everyone knew what the other person was doing. People of all age groups knew each other well.

My curiosity was all the more aroused when the other person swiftly gagged her and dragged her to the straw-stack and they were hidden from my view. I was at a loss. "What are they doing there?" I could not raise an alarm without knowing what they were doing. I was aware that even if I shouted no one would hear me. Her parents would be in their rice field at that moment for the ceremonial first ploughing of the year. Only her aged grandmother, who was hard of hearing, would be in their house. Both my parents were also away in school.

Eche-Nungshirei and the other person were at the straw-stack for quite a while. I kept wondering, what to do. Then I saw the other person running off arranging his *khudei*. He soon turned around the *mamang-sangoi* and was hidden from my view. I could never see his face. Not long after, her hair dishevelled and clothes loose, Eche-Nungshirei staggered out of the straw-stack and stood for a long time without caring to gather her clothes. I was dumbfounded to see her in that condition. I then heard her grandmother calling her and she started walking towards their house with unsteady steps. That was the last time I saw her.

After I passed class VI, my father was transferred to another school at Imphal and we left the village. On the day we left the village, I saw Ta-Tomchou through the window of the bus that was taking me away from the village. He was walking on the road with a limp. He seemed to have lost much of his physical strength, which I had not noticed earlier though I often went to their shop. At that moment a thought suddenly struck me, "Is he the man I saw with Eche-Nungshirei? Is God punishing him for his misdeed to her?"

Even after the lapse of more than thirty years, I could still recognize Eche-Nungshirei the moment I saw her. Age had weathered her face but her eyes had not lost much of the sparkle yet, white streaks showed here and there in her neatly combed hair tied in a bun at the back, still she could not be called a wizened old woman. The only thing that had not changed about her was her sweet voice. It was in a way fortunate for me that she did not recognize me. "How can she recognize me after all these years? She had known me as a small boy at the village."

She came with her husband to the hospital where I am working, for her daughter's treatment. Her daughter is a computer engineer. She also excels at various intellectual and athletic pursuits but she has started developing severe emotional disturbance and cognitive decline. She shows signs of involuntary movements. At times, she is obsessive and aggressive. After making rounds of the other departments in the hospital, her case was referred to me.

Both Eche-Nungshirei and her husband are very worried about their daughter, their only child. There is no evidence of any hereditary disease in the family history on Eche-Nungshirei's side. Nor is there any on her husband's side. But their daughter shows all the symptoms of Huntington's disease, a hereditary disease—a fatal, autosomal-dominant neurological illness. The only thing that can be done at the moment is to give her medicines to control her seizures, dystonia and myoclonus.

I am bogged down with the question, "Is the story of the incident that has been tormenting me for so long related with Eche-Nungshirei's daughter's life?" I shudder in agony, "How can I ever break the news about their daughter's illness to an unsuspecting Eche-Nungshirei and her unwary husband?"

I want to protect Eche-Nungshirei from the bad news—but for how long? Gradual disclosure may save her from a sudden jolt. Still, I have to tell her everything in the end. The news may devastate her.

Had I not known her I would have been spared of the pang deep inside my heart. I earnestly wish I had not witnessed the incident.

2

A strange admirer

February 14, 2002,
My Dearest,

Ah! Spring has arrived. Foggy mornings, chill winds, cold
wintry days—all are gone. The meadows with frost bitten dull-brown
dry grasses have put on a new light green carpet of tender shoots. Birds
once again perch on the branches of trees and start tweeting. Their long
forgotten melodious songs reverberate in the morning air. Floral buds
have sprouted on mango trees. Of all the fragrant and colourful flowers
why such an insignificant and dull flower like mango flower, you may
say. To me fragrance and colour carry no meaning—mango flower is the
loveliest of all the flowers. It reminds me of you.

The mango tree growing in your garden near the gate must be laden
with flowers, now. Yes, it is the floral buds of the same mango tree that
first made me aware of the astounding beauty of the spring—the first
spring of my life. At that time I was studying in the ninth class. I had
come to stay with my uncle at his house, a government quarter, for one
month only after my final examinations—my first stay in a town. He was
your next door neighbour.

The first morning at my uncle's place is still etched in my memory. I was startled by your shouts. You were trying to drive away small neighbourhood boys who had climbed up the mango tree to pull down a kite stuck there. They were spoiling the floral buds. You were angry. I came out, stood on the veranda and watched you with amusement. I was in awe—a sudden inexplicable chill crept over me. It is hard to explain what it was. I had never experienced such a feeling before. A chill running up my spine—it is not the same feeling one gets when one is frightened. It was rather a very pleasant chill. It drew me closer to you, and I watched you spellbound. Long after you had gone inside, I kept standing on the veranda eagerly waiting for you to come out again. But you didn't.

After that first meeting, no, seeing you for the first time may be more correct, I kept thinking about you. Even after such a long time your face still haunts me.

People say so much about the beauty of the spring, a time that not only brings to life the withered buds of trees but also rekindles the minds of young and old alike, with renewed hopes. Many a poet has sung the glory of spring; many a painter has frozen the beauty of spring on their canvases. But, none has been able to enliven spring as you have done. Poet's spring, painter's spring—all look dull and meaningless to me, who was born and grew up in a small village in nature's lap. You are the one who had awakened spring in my mind.

I spent the whole month at my uncle's place looking for an opportunity to speak to you. But, luck did not favour me. It may also be put this way that I did not have the courage even to go near you—a coward, I certainly am. I had to satisfy myself with a glimpse of you from a distance. Standing behind the window like a thief, I watched you every morning and evening when you came out of the house to tend your garden. Your garden, a wild splash of colours—beds of antirrhinum, calendula, phlox, nasturtium, gerbera, lupin and carnation all lending different hues; a honeysuckle climbing on an arch over the gate—I still remember vividly. But it was your presence that made the colour of your garden more vibrant.

While I was at my uncle's place, dark clouds hid the sky for three days and it rained continuously for two days—unexpected heavy spring shower. On those days also I stood behind the window waiting for you to come out. But you remained indoors. I cursed the weather for confining you inside the house. My imagination ran wild; I kept guessing what you might be doing inside.

My one-month stay flew by and the spring of my life came to an abrupt end. On the morning I left, the sun, a mellow morning sun, was shining brightly. I took a last look of your garden. The mango tree was in full bloom—light green floral buds had opened and turned pale cream, soon it would turn light brown before tiny green mangoes start peeping out. You were standing in its shade, admiring the pale cream bunches. And I saw a faint smile on your lips.

Physically, we are now miles apart but my mind is still very close to you. After completing my studies, I have taken up a job that keeps me on the other end of the country. Very often, my job keeps me on the move.

My uncle has long since left the house next to yours. After him many government officials, one after another, had occupied the quarter. During the last winter I went to my village to meet my parents. I broke my journey at Imphal for two days only to see you. On those two days, I walked past your house many times in the morning and evening. But you were nowhere to be seen. Once, I saw a girl in her early teens basking in the sun, sitting on a scooped plastic chair, with a book in her hand. I suppose she is your daughter. She is a carbon copy of you. She has inherited all your facial features the same eyes slanting upwards slightly at the corners, the same chiselled nose neither pointed nor snub but very sharp, the same hollow in the left cheek suggesting a faint dimple, the same round chin, the same lips neither thick nor thin and the same translucent flawless skin.

On my return journey, I saw you at the airport. All of a sudden, I sensed the same inexplicable chill I had felt when I saw you for the first time creeping over me. You were with your daughter. We were in the same aircraft flying from Imphal to Delhi. In the aircraft, you and your daughter sat in a row, two rows ahead of me. I was hoping that you would come to Delhi with me but you got off at Guwahati. After you had left I felt a strange emptiness in my mind as if my soul had followed you and only my physical self had been left behind. I could not concentrate on anything for days after that. I could neither sleep nor eat. I am still trying to recuperate my old self.

Your dimpled face with a charming smile has followed me wherever I go like my own shadow. However hard I try to forget, your face keeps appearing before me. I do not know what it is. Is it love-at-first-sight or physical attraction? No, it is neither of the two—with the difference in age between us it can never be. It is some sort of feeling more profound than both what people call love and physical attraction. May be, it is a different kind of love or emotional bond, which I am unable to explain. It seems to be some sort of sublime ecstasy. I want it to stay this way.

I no longer want to speak to you as I had yearned while I was staying with my uncle. I fear that once we start talking to each other it may become something the mortals do and shatter the image I have painstakingly conjured up in my mind. Still, I want myself to be heard. So, I have taken the liberty to write this letter. I do not want to hear back from you. I have not given my address. I wish to remain anonymous.

I am posting this letter from a place at the foot of the Himalayas that appears in my itinerary, a place where I am surrounded by mango trees laden with flowers of different hues—some light green, some pale cream and some brownish cream, all in different stages of opening. It is far off from the place where I stay.

Yours truly,
An admirer

*   *   *

In the evening, after the tiring household chores, Anuradha was resting on an easy chair on the veranda, reading the letter she had read over and over again during the last one year. Each time she read the letter, she became more perplexed. At the same time she also sensed a mild feeling of exhilaration. After she finished reading it, she folded it neatly and put it inside its old sweat-stained envelope.

She slowly turned her face to the garden—hers was the best garden in the whole of Babupara, a neighbourhood in Imphal. From the varieties of multicoloured flowers blooming in neat rows her eyes followed the direction towards the old mango tree growing near the gate. The last rays of the setting sun had painted its bunches of tiny pale cream flowers clustering on floral spikes orange—it looked aflame with orange flames leaping out in all directions. Spring had roused it from its deep slumber during the winter. The sight of the mango flowers sent a mild terror of shock in her mind.

She got up and moved slowly towards the gate. Suddenly she remembered, she had forgotten to check her mailbox. She peeped inside the mailbox. A lone envelope was lying there. She opened the mailbox and took it out. It was addressed to her—her name was typed in neat bold letters. But the sender had not given his or her name and address.

She took the envelope with her and went back to the easy chair. She examined the envelope carefully. No postage stamp was there. With a shaky hand she tore it open. Inside there was small piece of paper with only two neatly typed lines.

*   *   *

Imphal,
February 14, 2003

My Dearest,

Today morning, I saw you in your garden standing near the gate in the shade of the mango tree flowering profusely.

On this Valentine's Day, I send you my 'Heart'.

Yours truly,
An admirer

3

Ramu Prasad's Angel

A hot summer afternoon—not many people were out on the road, the fierce summer heat at its peak had confined everyone indoors. Only those who had to go on compulsion were out, clumsily walking on the road, with umbrellas to protect themselves from the glaring sun. 'Fire walking', walking swiftly over a layer of embers spread thinly along the bottom of a shallow trench, would in no case be less comfortable than walking on the heated asphalt.

In a dilapidated shack built next to the road, a washer-man's shop, dead tired after ironing all the clothes left in the morning, Ramu Prasad, a frail old man, was taking a nap to rest his weary bones. He was seeing a dream, flashback of the bygone days, of the days when he was younger . . .

On the bank of the Imphal River, he was sitting under the shade of a peepul tree, to cool off the summer heat, while waiting for the clothes he had spread out after washing to dry. His two children were prancing around merrily, unmindful of the scorching sun. The gaiety of their laughter filled the air. They saw a butterfly sitting on a wild rose and tried to catch it. The moment they held out their tiny hands it fluttered its colourful wings and flew off. They chased but it flew up and down, floating high up in air. It suddenly turned away and went almost out of sight. One of them ran to their father and pulled him hard holding his massive hairy right hand, crisscrossed with thick veins, with his tender hands and pleaded, "Please, catch the butterfly." . . .

All of a sudden, Ramu heard someone speaking to him very close to his ears, "Get up." A very sweet voice, though it gave him a sudden jolt.

"An angel speaking to me, I'm blessed!" he thought and winked his eyes to rub off sleep.

The voice continued, "Get up. Otherwise, I will turn you into a frog."

He sat up with a start and rubbed his eyes to clear. A small girl, not more than four, holding a stick in her hand, was standing near him, watching him intently with her sparkling dark brown eyes.

The moment she saw him awake, her innocent face turned serious and said, "Are you a stranger?"

Perplexed, Ramu exhaled a long breath and said with a toothless smile, "No, my sweet child, I'm not a stranger. I'm Ramu Prasad, your neighbourhood dhobi."

She tittered and said, "Good! My parents told me not to talk to strangers. But, what's a dhobi?"

"A washer-man."

"Then you're not a bad man. I'll turn all the bad men into frogs with my magic wand. They kidnap children."

"*Meri Pyari Pari*! What are you doing here? Where do you live?"

"*Meri Pyari Pari*," she repeated after him and said pointing to the big house with a well laid-out garden in front that could be seen through the small window of the shack, "I live there."

Ramu gently stroked her plump cheeks with his dry shrunken hands and said, "*Meri Pyari Pari*, so you live next-door. Won't your parents be worried when they find you missing?"

She chuckled and placed her forefinger before her pursed lips to hush him. She then whispered, "My parents are out. I have sneaked out while Nene is taking her siesta."

Ramu guessed, "Nene must be the maid who had brought clothes for ironing in the morning." He too lowered his voice and said, "Still, your Nene will be worried to find you missing when she wakes up. *Meri Pyari Pari*, go home, now."

"But, I want to play with you."

"*Meri Pyari Pari*, I have nothing to play with."

She looked around and thought for a while before pointing to the big heavy charcoal heated iron lying on the table that served as ironing board, "I want to play with it."

"Hai, Ram . . . Ram! It's not a plaything. It's hot and quite heavy."

She looked at him inquisitively and said, "What's it?"

With all the earnest to make her understand in the simplest way possible, he said, "It's my implement for ironing clothes."

"Will you iron my doll's clothes?"

"O yes *Meri Pyari Pari*."

"A promise?"

"Yes, a promise, *Meri Pyari Pari*."

"Tomorrow, I'll bring my doll's clothes."

Ramu was jubilant to learn that she would be coming again the next day but he was worried—she might go to school and be prevented from coming. He said, "Tomorrow? But, don't you go to school?"

"I go to school in the morning. I will come after school."

He said triumphantly, "Fine. See you tomorrow, then."

The small girl ran away happily, giggling all the while. She, an angel, had come and gone like the unpredictable spring clouds, one moment it was here, next moment it was gone and he was left alone brooding over his loneliness.

His forefathers belonged to the groups of people from Bihar who migrated to Assam in the wake of tea garden boom. Born and grew up at Dhubri, he had come to Imphal to seek his fortune after his marriage.

After the death of his wife, Ramu became very lonely; he worked harder and tried to keep himself busy to forget her. His work as a dhobi was all he knew and cherished. When his wife was alive he worked only to earn his livelihood and feed his family but after her departure it had become his friend, his companion, his love, his solace, his rest, his soul, his life, all in one. But, his sons would not allow him to do any work saying he was quite advanced in age and he needed rest. Without his work he was like a fish out of water.

One of his friends told him about the place at Airport road. The man who used to run a washer-man's shop in a shack had left and it was lying vacant. Without paying heed to his sons' request not to go there, he went there and opened his shop. He, who had never played with his grandchildren and avoided their company, unable to withstand the noise they made, had been overwhelmed by the small girl's openness. She, whose name even he did not know, except calling her lovingly '*Meri Pyari Pari*' or 'My Dear Angel' in Hindi his mother tongue, seemed to have brought a bit of sunshine to his turbulent life; her innocence had charmed and comforted him.

He pondered over the life of the small girl, "Poor little thing! She, such a sweet child, is the only child in the big house with no one to play with. Of course, her Nene is there but she would not want to play with her. She must be feeling very lonely . . ."

The following day, she came running, dragging along a bag. The moment she saw him, she giggled and said, "*Meri Pyari Pari*, here I am."

"Welcome, *Meri Pyari Pari*."

"See what I have brought for you," she said opening her bag and then brought out a bar of chocolate.

"Oh! Chocolate for me! No, you keep it."

She sulked at his refusal to accept what she had brought for him. She said, "Aren't you my friend?"

With a beaming smile on his face, he said, "You're mistaken. I'm your friend but I don't eat chocolate. It sticks to my teeth. What more have you got in your bag?"

She blushed and closed her bag, and hid it behind her back.

He tickled her and said, "No secret between friends. Right?"

She cackled with laughter and said, "Right. Stop tickling me."

She then opened her bag again and brought out a doll without any clothes on. "Shameless girl. She always gets her clothes dirty. I had to wash her clothes and hang it out to dry."

"Yesterday, you told me to iron your doll's clothes. Why didn't you bring it?"

With a twinkle in her eyes, she said, "But her clothes are not dry yet."

He said, "I can wash your doll's clothes and iron it too. Whenever, your doll's clothes are dirty bring it to me."

"But, I have never seen you washing clothes."

"*Meri Pyari Pari*, I told you I'm a dhobi. Washing clothes is my duty. I'm now old so I do not wash others' clothes. But, I will wash your doll's clothes."

She opened her eyes wide in wonder and said, "Good! So you also wash clothes."

Ramu, an old man, and the small girl had become inseparable friends. She would bring her dolls and toys, every day. She would think up new ways to play with her dolls and toys—'Going to market', 'Celebrating birthday', 'Going for picnic', 'Selling vegetables in the market', 'Going to school', . . . While playing, she would go on talking and ordering him to do this and that, "Keep the doll here . . . lay it down . . . put on new clothes . . . do the dishes . . .". He would never grouch and do whatever she said without a murmur. With her around, he did not notice how time had flown. She had brought spring in the autumn of his life.

Summer had gone, so too rainy season, followed by autumn. Winter had set in and the bond of friendship between the old man and his *Meri Pyari Pari* grew tighter.

Government machineries were busy with a plan for widening the roads in Imphal. Surveys were conducted. Many buildings and structures near the roads had to be pulled down to make room. Notices were served to the occupants to vacate and ultimatums were issued. Ramu Prasad's shack would have to go; there was no means of saving it. On the eve of New Year, his *Meri Pyari Pari* came as usual, her bag loaded with her dolls and toys. She was surprised to see her friend, old and frail Ramu, sitting dejectedly, all his belongings neatly packed and tied into a big bundle with a coarse white cloth.

She said, "*Meri Pyari Pari*, why are you looking so gloomy?"

Exhaling a long breath, he said with a pensive heart, "I am leaving tomorrow."

"Where?"

"Don't know."

"Won't you play with me now?"

A faint smile imprinted on Ramu's wrinkled face.

"O yes. How shall we play now?"

She brought out her doll and said, "Do you love my princess?"

Ramu could not help but laugh aloud, "Very much."

They then proceeded to play 'Princess and her magic wand'. With the magic wand the princess turned all the bad men into frogs . . .

When the time came for her to leave, she said, "When will you leave tomorrow?"

"Early in the morning."

Without any further query, she ran away leaving behind Ramu watching her till she vanished into her house.

The following morning she sneaked out through the backdoor, went around their house, opened the gate without making any noise and came out. Once out of the gate she ran to the shack where Ramu was waiting for her.

Still panting, she gave him a small packet, a parting gift, wrapped with old newspaper.

"What's this?"

"Open it later."

Both of them faintly heard her mother calling her for breakfast, in the distance.

She turned around and said, "Mama is calling me."

She did not stay even a moment longer to say good-bye, she rushed off like a flash of lightning in a dark stormy night that momentarily shone to show everything only to engulf all in darkness the next moment.

After she had left, Ramu opened the packet with shaky hands. A sense of mild exhilaration filled his mind; his heart ached with the pang of separation. Inside was a doll, her princess of the previous day, the one he had said he loved.

Holding the doll in his right hand, with his left hand Ramu lifted the bundle packed with his belongings and started walking slowly with his frail legs—the start of a new year, a new beginning, a new destination, another new chapter of his life.

4

The Prophecy

I t was a moonless night. Kanta, a small-time thief, was speeding alone fast on his bike, a sleek red Hero Honda, along a long stretch of a deserted road leading away from Puri beach after disposing of his booty at a clandestine shop on the beach, dealing in stolen goods. Except for the light thrown by the headlight of his bike, it was frighteningly dark all around. The gentle breeze from the sea started breaking into a fierce storm. The wind picked up speed howling loudly and tried to blow away everything in its path, showing its destructive power. Lightning flashed across the dark turbulent sky illuminating the whole area for a fraction of a second, followed by the loud booming roar of thunder.

He had covered about eight kilometres or so inland when it started raining. Raindrops as big as grapes poured down incessantly. He still had a long way to go. With the high velocity raindrops jabbing at his face continuously, he found it difficult to keep his eyes open. He looked around for a safe place to take shelter till the rain stopped. He cursed himself for having avoided the main highway as there was no need to worry about the police on his return journey without the booty. A little ahead in the beam of his bike's hazy headlight the outline of a small white structure, unmistakably that of a roadside temple appeared.

"It is strange. I have travelled along this road many times but I have never seen this temple," he thought, *"Maybe I was too preoccupied to notice."*

He immediately applied the brake and the bike screeched to a stop. After parking it, he ran to the temple. As he climbed the steps, he heard a serene and gentle voice welcoming him, clearly above the roar of wind.

"Come in, Kanta. I knew you would come. I have been waiting for you."

He suddenly realised that he was not alone but could not see who the other person was. Lightning flashed again. In the momentary flood of light, he was taken aback to see a Sadhu whom he had never met before, sitting in *padmasana* posture. He was naked except for a small piece of cloth covering his groin.

"Don't be afraid. Come closer my child," continued the Sadhu.

Kanta groped in the darkness and knelt down near him without uttering a word.

"Now, listen to me carefully. I have a very important advice for you to follow."

He paused briefly waiting for Kanta's reply. Puzzled at the mysterious happening; a Sadhu, a complete stranger out of the blue, calling him by name, Kanta did not say anything but simply nodded his head.

"I am afraid, the path you are leading is wrong but there is still time to correct."

The Sadhu's well-meaning words caught Kanta unaware. He felt blood suddenly rushing to his face. He blushed with shame as if he had been caught with his pants down in public. All the precautions he had taken to cover up his job of stealing had failed to deceive the omniscient Sadhu.

"If you don't realise your mistakes and mend your ways, you would die an unnatural death."

Kanta could not remain silent any longer. His inquisitiveness got the better of him, "*Baba*, what should I do to undo my past mistakes?"

"It is very simple my child. You devote your remaining life in the service of the poor and downtrodden. I am sure it will not be difficult for you."

"I promise to do whatever you tell me."

"You start by distributing your ill-gotten wealth to the poor and needy."

"I swear I will do just that."

"I warn you, my child, if you fail to keep your promise you will die at the hands of a child who is born long after the death of both his parents."

After giving the warning, the Sadhu stopped talking. Kanta also maintained a respectful silence. With his eyes now adjusted to the darkness, he could clearly see the intricate carvings of exceptional beauty on the inner walls of the temple in the light thrown by a strange glow radiating from the Sadhu. The rain did not last long. The ferocious wind also slowed down to cool and refreshing breeze. Slowly, the sky cleared to show the stars twinkling above.

With folded hands Kanta bowed his head to pay his respects and show his gratitude to the Sadhu. After that, he left the temple and went home.

The next day, he returned to the same road looking for the roadside temple where he had taken shelter the previous night. He drove his bike to and fro along the full stretch of the deserted road again and again but the temple was nowhere to be seen.

After his unfruitful trip he proceeded to the new township, a booming commercial centre, on the outskirts of Bhubaneshwar. The repeated to and fro drive along the long deserted road made him hungry. He went to a fast-food joint to take a quick bite to ease his hunger. The strange Sadhu's still stranger prophecy, *"You will die at the hands of a child who is born long after the death of both his parents"* was lingering in his mind and made him restless. Sitting on a revolving stool next to the footpath, munching a burger he idly looked around. On the opposite side of the wide road he saw a four-storied modern glass and steel building standing in the middle of a spacious well laid-out and carefully manicured garden. Placed above the main entrance of the building was a huge sign, 'HOPE NURSING HOME'.

A young couple came out through the majestic sliding glass-front-door. Even from such a long distance, his experienced eyes could pick out the pair of diamond earrings the woman was wearing. His interest was suddenly aroused. His eyes followed the couple. The couple hopped in a small imported Japanese-car, just the right size to squeeze through the busy city traffic, parked in the parking lot and drove off. He had forgotten all about the Sadhu's prophecy. He came out of the fast-food joint and followed the car on his bike. The car entered a posh residential area with beautiful houses on both sides of the road and parked in the driveway of an eye-catching bungalow with neatly trimmed hedges all around, demarcating the boundary of compound. He noted down the address, "3, Road C, Unit 8, Gopabandhu Nagar" carefully and returned home.

Late in the night when everyone was sleeping peacefully, he went to the posh residential area. He did not find any difficulty in locating the young couple's house. He broke into the house. When he was about to leave after clearing all the valuables, the couple woke up and tried to raise alarm. He jumped on the helpless husband and wife; and murdered them mercilessly before making good his escape. After that, there was no looking back.

It all had happened about five years ago. Kanta was now a renowned figure. He had a dual-personality like the two sides of a coin. He was covertly the powerful leader of an underworld Mafia gang who wore the mask of a generous kind-hearted peace-loving citizen. To the common man he was a rich man who owned a chain of departmental stores but his real income was from the clandestine night-clubs and gambling dens his gang operated.

His rise to power was phenomenal. The Sadhu's prophecy had given him the courage. He reasoned, *"How can a child be born long after the death of his parents? Impossible."* He easily fought his way to the top. He knew that he would come out of the fights unscathed because his killer would never be born. He overpowered and silenced many contenders for the coveted position without much difficulty. He visited temples regularly and distributed alms to the beggars crowding there, to project his image as a pious man and deceive the unsuspecting people of the city. His generosity and kindness towards the poor and needy populace of the city had elevated him to the superlative position of a Demigod and earned the title "Data-Kanta", *data* meaning 'generous'.

With the rival Mafia gangs logged in never-ending war of supremacy, Kanta's life was supposed to be in constant danger but he roamed around freely without the retinue of bodyguards; unlike the leaders of the other gangs. He was sure that his rivals could never kill him. His only problem was people recognising him wherever he went. As a man of prominence, he could do nothing in public places without being mobbed by the people present there. His life was like an open book for everyone to see. He longed to roam around carefree in public places as a common man and spend some time on his own without others recognising and disturbing him.

He planned meticulously to fulfil his desire. On the eve of *Holi*, he sent away all his servants and immediate employees serving in his house on a long holiday after paying them generous sums of money. After everyone had left, he took out his secret paraphernalia. He put on a grey wig with matching false grey moustache, donned spotless white *dhoti* and *kurta*; and added a pair of spectacles with plain glass to his costume to make the picture in his mind complete. He stood before the mirror and looked at the old man in front of him with satisfaction, "*Even my next-door neighbour would not be able to recognise me in the disguise.*"

He stealthily came out of the house with a walking stick in his hand. He crossed the road in front of his house and walked on. He proceeded to a nearby market and entered a crowded departmental store owned by him. He wasted a good hour there, watching with humour the endless stream of customers hurrying through the different sections to make their purchases and the salespersons helping them. No one recognised him. He felt like an escaped cage-bird free to soar in the vast open sky anywhere in any direction. As he came out he collided with a woman hurrying out of the store after buying everything she needed till she could carry no more. She slipped on the road scattering all her packages around her.

He apologised and helped her to get up. She was on the verge of losing her nerve but soon controlled herself when she saw that the person with whom she had collided was an old harmless looking man. He picked up the packages and offered to take her to her house in a taxi. She reluctantly agreed when he told her that he belonged to a remote village and was a newcomer to the city. He had come to the city only for a week to meet his son who worked in the departmental store.

He hailed a taxi and they got in. Throughout their ride in the taxi they remained silent. The taxi stopped at the address given by her. She lived in a fourth floor flat all by herself. After getting down from the taxi she paid the fare. He helped her to carry the packages up to her flat. When he was about to leave after putting down the last of the packages at her door, she invited him to come inside for a cup of tea. It was a very neat and tidy two-room flat. He sat on a comfortable couch and looked around the room while she prepared tea in the kitchen. The furniture and decor showed that she had an artistic taste. On the opposite wall hung an enlarged photograph of her cuddling a baby, encased in a highly polished expensive brass frame.

She brought an exquisite ivory-white hand painted fine-china tea set with crafted silver spoons, two empty cups and saucers; and a plate of delicious looking home-made cookies on a silver tray. She placed the tray on a walnut tea table with carved legs that showed fine craftsmanship. When she poured out tea into the empty cups, the room was suddenly filled with the unmistakable aroma of garden-fresh hand-picked choicest Darjeeling-tea.

She held up a cup and asked, "Milk? Sugar?"

"I prefer tea without milk and sugar to get the real flavour. Honestly, at my humble place I can't always afford milk and sugar."

She opened her eyes wide in surprise, "Really! I also take tea the same way. It is very un-Indian but I think milk and sugar spoil the real taste of tea. I keep milk and sugar for visitors though anyone seldom drops in."

Kanta now felt comfortable enough to inquire about the photograph on the wall, "Your baby?"

"Yes and no."

"I couldn't get you."

She elaborated, "The baby grew up in my womb and was delivered by me but I am not the real mother."

"I still couldn't get you. You are puzzling me more."

She suddenly became serious. She took a deep breath and gave a weary sigh.

"I haven't disclosed this to anyone around here but I see no harm in telling you the whole story. It will relieve me of the great burden of keeping it a secret for such a long time."

She narrated her heartfelt story to an attentive Kanta. She grew up in an orphanage and was trained as a nurse. She worked at a private hospital, HOPE NURSING HOME, which catered to the needs of the affluent section of the city. She longed to settle down to a peaceful family life. But who would come forward to tie the nuptial knot with someone who was brought up in an orphanage?

About five years ago, a very jovial and friendly young childless couple, Mr. and Mrs. J.C. Das, came to the nursing home. They were eager to have a child of their own. Mrs. Das had the problem of blocked fallopian tubes, which was the root-cause of their problem. They visited the nursing home a number of times to extract mature and healthy eggs from her ovaries. The eggs were then fertilised with her husband's sperms in a dish containing a special medium or fluid—test-tube baby. The fertilised eggs were kept frozen for depositing in her womb later on.

She was secretly drawn towards Mr. J.C. Das, the handsome husband and had a hidden desire to mother his child. A very unfortunate turn of events ended the lives of the young bright couple. Their wealth became their enemy. Their house was ransacked and stripped of all the valuables; and they were murdered in their own bedroom.

All of a sudden Kanta blurted out, "Mr. and Mrs. J.C. Das of 3, Road C, Unit 8, Gopabandhu Nagar?"

"Precisely. How did you know?" There was a hint of surprise in her voice.

Kanta realised he had given himself away. His quick wit came to his rescue.

"A generous couple. My son worked in their jewellery shop for some time before he joined the departmental store. I had visited their house with my son on two occasions in connection with loan for my daughter's marriage. It was only because of their kindness that I could arrange my daughter's marriage."

She had swallowed his story. She did not suspect anything wrong. She continued with her narration. Mr. Das was the only child of his parents. His father was also a rich man who stayed in another Metropolitan City where he owned a chain of jewellery shops. It was at his insistence that Mr. Das came to the city and opened his own jewellery shop. His father wanted him to learn the trade on his own so that he could expand the business and would not find any problem to manage the chain of jewellery shops, he would inherit one day.

Sr. Das, Mr. Das's father came to know about the frozen fertilised eggs deposited at the nursing home about a year after his precious son's death. His shattered hope of propagating the lineage of his family to the future was rekindled. The moment he learnt about the eggs, he dashed down to the nursing home and inquired about revitalising them. She met him at the nursing home and offered to take the role of a surrogate mother. By becoming the surrogate mother her two secret desires, to be a mother and to mother Mr. Das's child, which she had been yearning for a long time would be fulfilled.

After consulting her employer it was settled, she could be the surrogate mother and all the maternity benefits given to the employees of the nursing home would be availed to her. The terms and conditions put by Sr. Das were "After the implantation of the embryo in her womb she has to stay at the nursing home under the direct supervision of the doctors till the delivery of the baby. The baby would be handed over to him after the baby starts weaning on to semi-solid food. Till that time she has to stay at a place of his choice." She accepted the terms and conditions. The doctors at the nursing home were also very happy to learn that one of their nurses would be the surrogate mother.

When asked, she refused to name her price. However, Sr. Das presented her a well-furnished flat and deposited a fat balance in her account at the bank.

"The baby in the photograph is Mr. Das's son. He stays with his grandfather. I get a chance to meet him once every year when Sr. Das brings him here to celebrate his birthday. He is now exactly three years old. Today is his birthday. I was at the departmental store to buy presents for him. They will come to pick me up. I am expecting them any moment now."

Kanta was gripped by a sudden terror. He was bathed in cold sweat to learn that his terminator had already been born. He lamented silently, *"How foolish I have been not to take the Sadhu's advice! I have been blinded by my greed for the riches. Now, I cannot escape my destiny. I will die at the hands of an innocent boy who has been brought to this world long after the death of his parents to finish me off."*

She noticed his off-colour face and the drops of sweat on his forehead. She inquired, "Something wrong? Not feeling well?"

"Nothing wrong. I'm fine."

She heard him but she was really concerned about the sudden change that had come over him, "Are you sure, you're all right?"

He got up to leave and said, "There is nothing wrong with me. I have to take leave of you now. Thank you so much for the hospitality."

"I'll come up to the road to see you off."

Closing the door gently behind him, he said, "Please don't bother."

He went to the lift. It was going up. He pushed the call-button and waited for the lift to come down. More than five minutes had passed but the lift was still not coming down. Every second seemed like a year to him. It seemed that the ticking of each second was bringing his end closer. His heart was pounding fast; his terminator was due to arrive any moment now. He did not want to die so soon. He had to escape from the place and go to a far off place to buy time. The sound of a car parking below near the entrance of the building frightened him out of his wits.

"My terminator has arrived. He will be coming up in the lift. I cannot use the lift now. I shall use the stairs instead."

He went to the stairs and started running down. When he was about to reach the last landing an apparition appeared before him. A man with his long mottled and knotted hair tied tightly in a bun on the top of his head was standing at the landing with his arms extended as if to welcome him. He was naked except for a small piece of cloth covering his groin. The man was no other than the Sadhu of the roadside temple.

Kanta tried to stop running but lost his balance. He slipped and went headlong down the flight of steps and landed with a thud on the ground. When he came to his senses he was lying on a bed in hospital. He lifted his right hand with great difficulty and felt around his head and face. His wig and false moustache were still intact. He felt a great relief.

"So they have not yet noticed my disguise."

He faintly heard a nurse informing someone that the patient had come around. A doctor came to inform him that he was not badly hurt; he would be on his feet in a day or so. The doctor soon left.

Kanta, wreathing with numbing pain all over his body, closed his eyes. After a while he heard someone calling him softly, "Please open your eyes and see who have come."

He slowly opened his eyes and saw a nurse standing near him. The nurse moved aside so that he could see the visitors. What he saw made him gap his jaw with awe. The surrogate mother of his terminator and an old man with a child, a small boy, in his arms, were standing behind the nurse.

The surrogate mother came closer and said, "How are you feeling? Sr. Das and his grandson are with me. We brought you to Hope Nursing Home for treatment in his car. You were lucky. He had just arrived with his grandson when you slipped down the stairs."

He got a terrible and frightening shock to learn that his terminator was present. He slipped back into semi-consciousness. He was faintly aware of Sr. Das coming closer with his grandson still in his arms. He was asking his grandson to feel the patient's forehead as gesture of good wishes. No, Sr. Das was not holding the child; through his hazy eyes Kanta saw the Sadhu holding the child in his arms.

The child extended his hand and his tiny fingers gently touched the patient's forehead. The touch gave Kanta the final blow that sent him to the metaphysical land of no return.

5

Feline Guest in My Den

Softly humming a song, Imo was leisurely climbing the stairs leading to his place, a two-room flat on the fifth floor, which he intimately called "My Den". He did not bother to use the lift. He had plenty of time to kill. He was planning to go to bed late and sleep till 9:00 a.m.—getting up late, a luxury he had earned after working hard for five days of the week. There would be enough time to have a quick breakfast before catching the 10:00 a.m. train to the seaside resort. He badly needed some time to relax on his own. The idea of escaping from his mechanical life to loiter around the beach in gay abandon the whole weekend fascinated him.

After the tiresome journey back from his place of work, in a crowded bus, he had gone to the neighbourhood restaurant run by a homely Chinese couple, his favourite eatery and took his dinner; white cloud-ears soup, steamed fish, fried rice and pork cooked with preserved bamboo-shoot. He gulped and drained down everything into his small stomach with chilled beer. After the heavy meal he could barely move. He dragged himself to the public park across the road. There, he sat on a bench and wasted a good hour, watching the passers-by. Fresh air in the park refreshed him.

He, a newcomer to the neighbourhood, a large well-planned residential complex dotted with public parks and playgrounds quite a distance from the old city, had no one known to him except a Chinese couple, the owners of a restaurant. When he first moved in, they mistook him for a Chinese because of his mongoloid features common to north-east Indians. The first time he went to the restaurant, the husband came out from his permanent place behind the counter and greeted him with a wide satisfied beaming smile. He called out his wife from the kitchen where she was personally supervising the preparation of the delicacies to be served to the customers. The couple bowed their heads, in their traditional way of welcoming an honoured guest. They offered him a comfortable table near the window with a good view of the public park across the road. Imo realised the reason of the special attention given to him, only when the husband spoke to him in Chinese. To his unaccustomed ears it sounded strange. He politely informed them that he was not a Chinese but a native from the north-eastern part of India.

He was still humming a song jovially when he put the key into the keyhole of his flat's door. Out of nowhere, a cat came and nudged against his legs. It was purring softly in tune with the song on his lips. He thumped his left foot to drive it away. It moved back a little and kept watching him as if nothing had happened. Furious at the unconcerned nature of the cat, he shouted aloud and thumped his right foot again and again.

The door of the next flat opened and a woman wearing white cotton sari with broad maroon borders came out—the first meeting with his neighbour. She watched him inquisitively without a word. Her wide questioning eyes told him that she was annoyed at the noise he was making. He did not want to give her a wrong impression at the first meeting. He pointed to the cat and told her that he was only trying to drive it away. She neither moved nor uttered a sound; she simply kept staring. Her silence made him feel uneasy. He turned the key and opened the door. The cat moved swiftly and darted in before the door was closed. Once inside, it quickly jumped on the top of a cupboard and stayed there.

Imo pulled a chair and climbed on it. He reached his hands out to catch the cat. It bared its teeth and gave a warning touch-me-not meow. He thought of a way to woo it to come down. He poured out a little milk into a saucer and held it up for the cat to see.

"Tom! Come down and have milk."

Without realising he had given the cat a name, 'Tom'. He then placed the saucer on the floor and waited a long time for the cat to come down but it held its ground on the top of the cupboard. Tired, he put out the light and went to bed. He soon fell asleep.

He was woken up by a movement in his bed. He was scared and felt around with his right hand. He touched something very soft, which made his hairs stand erect with fright. He immediately put on the bedside lamp. He heaved a sigh of relief when he saw the cat near him. He looked at the table clock.

"It is only one O' clock. So, I have slept only for half an hour."

Furious at disturbing his sleep he kicked the cat hard. With a loud terrifying meow, it went flying in air and landed on the floor softly on four. It was now the cat's turn to be frightened. It ran around the room looking for a safe place to hide. It jumped up on the table and pushed down the hand-painted flower vase, Imo's prize possession. The porcelain vase crashed on the floor and shattered into pieces.

Then the cat climbed up the window curtain. Imo realised it would be futile to try to chase it away. The best thing would be to wait patiently till it came over the fright. He sat on the bed and watched it silently. After a while, he stretched out on the bed and closed his eyes but could not sleep at all. When the soft rays of the early morning sun filtered through the partially open blind and fell on his face, he got up and took a bath. All his plans about getting up late had been shattered.

He felt sorry for the starving cat. He quickly dressed and went out after locking the front door. He left the bathroom window wide open hoping that the cat would leave through it. He caught a bus to the market. There, he took his breakfast at a road-side restaurant and roamed around for a while. The shops started opening one by one. Half-heartedly, he went inside a big departmental store, which stocked pet-food. Still wishing to find the cat gone when he returned, he bought a month's supply of cat-food and came back.

When he opened the door of his flat and went inside, he was greeted by the cat with a soft meow. It came running and nudged against his legs. It had come over the initial fright.

Imo had completely forgotten his plans for the weekend. He found an empty cardboard box and put a soft cushion in it to make a comfortable bed for the cat. It scrutinised its new bed. First, it extended its front right paw and touched the cushion—soft, perfect to its liking. It then jumped into the box and stretched out with a satisfied purr.

Tom had brought a welcome change to Imo's lonely life. Tom had changed now from *it* to *he*, Imo's friend. Imo made it a point to return straight to his "My Den" after work to play with Tom. He played with Tom and talked to *him*, whenever he was home. Tom turned out to be a good listener—*he* always listened to Imo's extended monologues attentively, never disturbing him except for occasional meows to encourage him. Before leaving for work he would open the bathroom window and keep it open to enable Tom to go out and roam around the building. He hated to keep anyone in confinement, he considered, "Freedom is the most precious thing in life!"

One Monday, Imo was about to leave for an important meeting. He opened the door and came out. Tom followed him outside. A poodle came running, barking ferociously. Frightened, Tom ran down the stairs. Imo called out frantically but *he* never turned back. His neighbour came running and picked up the poodle. She then opened the door of her flat and went inside without a word. He also left hurriedly.

When he returned home in the evening after office, Tom was missing. He was calling out loudly and searching for Tom when his doorbell rang—a great surprise.

"Who may be there? I am not expecting anyone. I do not know anyone around here."

He opened the door only to find a girl, a complete stranger, standing outside. She gracefully nodded her head making her long black silky tresses sway gently. Sparkling doe-eyes, smooth golden-brown skin, thin but sensuous full lips slightly curved at the corners to convey an enchanting smile—her captivating beauty had completely charmed him. His heart raced wildly. A strange sense of helplessness, which he had never felt before had come over him—a stunned prey about to be devoured by a python. Not knowing what to say, he stood spellbound without a word. It took him a while to compose himself.

"Err . . . err . . . can I help you?"

"I am Sonali . . . Sonali Dasgupta, your neighbour. My mother told me that Furry . . . ah . . . ah . . . our dog had chased away your cat. Has it come back?"

"No, Tom hasn't come back. Don't worry. I am sure *he* can easily find *his* way back."

"I'm sorry. It was all Furry's fault."

"By the way, I am Imo Singh from Manipur. I work in a Multi-national Company. I live here alone."

"Now that we know each other, why don't you come over to our place for a cup of tea?"

He could not resist the tempting invitation.

"I'll have a quick wash and come."

After closing the door, he immediately went into the bathroom and took a quick shower—a cold water bath in the evening on a hot summer day after travelling in a crowded bus. He felt refreshed as if he had suddenly been transported to Heaven from Hell. He changed into a clean casual dress and went to her place. She was waiting for him. He met her parents. They were also newcomers. They had moved in only one month ahead of him. He had a long conversation with the family, covering various topics ranging from culture to politics. The invitation for tea turned into invitation for dinner. Sonali's mother prepared fried brinjal, stuffed tomato, roti, dal, plain rice and fish curry. He ate his plate clean. After dinner, sweet curd and *rasgoola* were served. He stuffed himself till he could not swallow any more. After that day, Imo started visiting Sonali's family whenever he felt lonely. They especially Sonali's mother also looked forward to his visits. She loved talking to him, a good listener.

Dead tired after a hectic day at the office, one night Imo was preparing to go to bed early. His doorbell rang. Silently, he cursed the visitor for disturbing him at such an odd hour. He opened the door and faced Sonali, directly. On seeing her smiling face his tiredness had suddenly vanished.

"Imo-da, come over to our place. I have something to show you."

Charmed Imo could not refuse her eager but innocent invitation. He quietly followed her after closing the door. What she wanted to show him turned out to be a harmonium, which she had left behind at their ancestral house in Kolkata. Knowing her love for it, her uncle had sent it to her. She made him sit on an easy-chair while she took her position behind the harmonium. Her parents came and sat beside her. With her left hand she started moving the back flap of the harmonium forward and backward to pump air while her perfectly sculptured nimble right-hand fingers followed the keys. He had never noticed before how beautifully sculptured her fingers were.

She sang a Rabindra Sangeet, "*Kee gabo aami, kee sunabo aajee aanando dhame* (What shall I sing, what shall I offer for listening to the exuberant gathering of today) . . ." to the accompaniment of the harmonium. He slowly drifted along the steady flow of the song. Her sweet voice carried him away and soon transported him to a surrealistic world of sublime ecstasy. He was still suspended in an allegorical world of his own when he left her place after the song.

After coming back to his place, he went straight to bed but could not close his eyes. Unable to sleep, he got up and went out to the small balcony. Down below, headlights of fast moving vehicles had joined hands with rows of blazing street lamps, in fighting the darkness of the night. High above in the clear moonless dark sky, stars twinkled, the same stars that could be visible at his distant home in the north-eastern corner of the country. The twinkling light of the tiny stars seemed to be conveying a silent coded-message from home. Rabindra Sangeet, barely audible, in Sonali's melodious voice wafted about, *"Akash-bhora surjo-tara, biswa-bhora pran* (Sky laden with Sun and stars, Universe laden with souls) . . ."

"How fortunate she is! She has brought a part of Bengal with her. She may be far away from home but she has transformed her flat into a Little Bengal—a home away from home."

"Here, I am standing alone in the dark. All the links with my roots have been severed—a faceless man in the ocean of multitude of humans."

"How I miss Tom! In this distant land, *his* meow is the only sound closest to my mother tongue. His meows transcend the barrier of languages."

It was well past midnight when he went to bed again. After that day, he had not met Sonali for a long time since he had to go on tour to complete a new job-assignment. When he returned, he met Sonali and her parents as they were coming out of the lift that he was waiting to go up. It was Sonali who spoke first.

"Imo-da! I was worried. You had vanished without a trace."

"I'm sorry. I didn't inform you. I had to go to another town and stay there for a while to complete some urgent work."

"Tomorrow is Sunday. We are going to the seaside resort for picnic. We will leave early in the morning and be back late in the evening. We have already engaged a taxi to go there. Now, we are going out to buy a few things for the picnic."

Sonali's mother joined in. "We want you also to come along."

Her mother's invitation gave her courage. She insisted Imo to come with them. They left after extracting a promise from him to join the picnic.

Imo was jubilantly humming a song when he put the key into the keyhole. On opening the door he was greeted with a meow. Tom was there on Imo's bed but *he* was not alone. Three kittens were prancing around on the bed. They had torn the bed-sheet into shreds. Even the mattress was torn at places. The flat was in a complete mess. He remembered the bathroom window always kept open to let Tom in.

He gave a weary sigh and murmured, "So, Tom is a *she*."

6

The Second Death of Oinam Rabei

The dark blue hills in the west had almost completely swallowed the setting Sun. The western sky was patches of scarlet, orange, dark grey, white and different shades of blue. Had a painter earnestly copied the cloud mottled evening sky on his canvas, it would have been described as a surrealistic scene, unrealistic use of colours, the height of wild imagination, contrary to his honest depiction of nature. Some critics would even brand it as an abstract painting. But, there it was a reality, right in front of me as I was riding homewards on my scooter following a road cut by the side of a hill. Astound as I was at the breathtaking beauty of the kaleidoscopic display, for a brief moment I had completely forgotten my physical self, an organic being, a human—very much part and parcel of nature.

Halfway home from Changamdabi as I crossed a thickly populated village and struck the highway running through vast open paddy fields, it started raining without any warning. I was not prepared. There was still a long way to go but I had not brought my mack. Soon, it would be dark. I already soaked from head to toe, tried to drive through the rain but could not go any farther than half a kilometre. The rain became heavier and fell in torrents. I found it really hard to keep my eyes open and looked around for a place to take shelter till the rain stopped or thinned down to drizzle. A little ahead, I saw a bus-waiting shed at the junction where a country road leading from a village met the highway. Keeping my eyes half closed to keep off the watery onslaught, I made for the shed and tried to park my scooter close to it.

"Oh! You're completely drenched."

I felt a sudden chill running up my spine at the unexpected female voice. I turned around and saw an old woman packing her things in a corner of the shed. After parking my scooter I ran to the shed.

"Yes, I'm dripping. Nowadays, the weather is so uncertain. The sky was spotlessly clear when I left home in the morning. Never expected, it would rain so heavily, today."

"How far do you have to go, *Son?*"

"I've to go to Athokpam."

"You still have to go quite a distance."

"It's hardly fifteen to twenty minutes' drive from here. *Ema,* what're you doing here alone at such an odd hour? I hope you aren't waiting for a bus. The last bus on this route must have left already."

"No, I'm not waiting for a bus. I've set up a stall here and sell home-made munchies and a few other things to earn my living. Life hasn't been so smooth after the death of my son, my only child."

"I'm so sorry."

Absorbed in our own thoughts, both of us remained silent and watched intently the incessant downpour. After a while, my inquisitiveness got the better of me.

"How did your son die?"

"It is a long story. My son was employed in a government office. He met a fatal accident while working. Only after his death, I came to know, he had been working as a ghost."

"I don't wish to be rude or put you in an embarrassing situation but it sounds interesting. Please do tell me about your son."

"There's no harm in telling the story. On the other hand, it'll lighten my burden of keeping it a secret for such a long time. I've met no one who'll listen to me and understand the complexity of the story."

The woman narrated her sorrowful story. She became a widow at an early age. She toiled day and night to bring up and educate her son. After her son had graduated from college, she thought that her problem would be over but she was wrong. Her son appeared in a number of interviews for a government job but he was never selected as they did not have enough money to pay the underhand price as the trend demanded.

"One day, all of a sudden, someone whom my son had met during his pursuit of a government job, came to our house. He was said to be working as a clerk in a government office at Thoubal. They had a long chat but I had no idea what they were conspiring with each other. After he had left, my son told me that luck had favoured him. By the grace of God, he would be able to get a job for the down payment of a small sum."

With great difficulty, she managed to arrange the required sum and secured the job for her son. She was not aware of the exact nature of his work. Most of the time, he had to stay at Senapati, away from home.

"My son was engaged in some sort of construction and travelled all over the hills in Senapati District. I was left alone in the house, dreaming of his marriage, my daughter-in-law and my grandchildren. Alas, all my dreams were short-lived!"

She remained silent for a long time but I did not have the courage to nudge her to continue the story. Her watery eyes told me everything. I could very easily guess what was going on deep inside her mind. She was trying to control and overcome the anguish of separation from her son, the sole hope of her future. I couldn't help but wonder, '*Separation from someone near and dear is always very difficult to bear. How can a mother so easily forget her departed son and quench the fire burning deep within*'

She continued her story with a shaky voice drowned in melancholy.

"Even before the first year of his employment was completed, the news of his fatal accident was brought. I was on the verge of losing my sanity but managed to put myself together with great difficulty. Someone told me that I would get some monetary benefits if I claimed as my son had died while working. I decided to stack the claim and donate whatever amount I would get to construct a building for the primary school in our village so that his name would shine forever."

She abruptly stopped her story and noisily took several long breaths while trying to control her emotion. Unable to coax her to continue, I remained a silent spectator. She dried the corners of her eyes and wiped her face with the loose end of the cloth wrapped on her upper body. She then inhaled deeply and poured out the remaining portion of the story.

"Whirlwind of events, that followed my son's demise sent me from one office to another, ultimately to the head office and made me a destitute, the mother of a non-existent person. I, an illiterate person, still cannot make out head or tail of what the people at the head office had told me. Now, I wish that I had never claimed the benefits."

"What did they tell you?"

"My son had been working at Thoubal. He died in a tragic accident, months before he actually met the fatal accident at Senapati."

"I can't grasp the meaning. Please tell me everything they said."

"When I reached the head office along with the papers forwarded from the place of my son's posting, I was told that it was impossible. As per the records available there, one Oinam Rabei had been transferred from Thoubal to Senapati but he died before he could join his new place of posting."

"What's the relation between your son and this Oinam Rabei?"

"Oinam Rabei is the name of my son."

"But, your son died while working at Senapati?"

"His joining the office at Senapati is not in the records at the head office. He was a ghost. A single person can neither work at a different place after his death nor die a second time."

I did not bother to ask her any more questions. She hurriedly put her small packages into a big bamboo basket and said, "I want to be home before it's completely dark. I'm leaving now as I've to walk a long distance. *Son*, you wait here till the rain stops."

I helped her to lift the basket and place it on her head. After opening an umbrella, she stepped out in the rain with the basket balanced on her head and started walking with quick strides. In the rain-washed failing light, she soon turned into a small shadowy figure in the distance. I watched her till she merged with the hazy background and completely vanished from my sight. I was left alone with questions lingering in my mind.

"Was her son really a ghost?"

"Or, did he die for the second time?"

". . . No, neither of the two can be true. Then?"

"Could he have been a victim of fake appointment plaguing government departments?"

7

A Pair of broken Spectacles

A clear mid-summer-day afternoon in the sub-tropical region is a time not to remain out of doors even by mistake especially for those who have the habit of working under the roof. Sitting inside a cauldron placed over smouldering fire would be more comfortable in comparison. But, it was exactly what Maipak, a computer programmer who seldom left his workstation, experienced one Sunday afternoon. Unexpected but compelling circumstances had brought him to the isolated open place where a long dusty road leading from Toubul, a lovely village on the shore of the Loktak Lake met the highway after passing through paddy fields. Braving the scorching sun, he had been waiting alone for a bus that would take him back to the comfort of his home.

From where he was standing, he could clearly see the long stretch of the deserted highway in both the directions to his left and right. That day being a Sunday, the buses on the usually busy highway took their own time to transport the fewer number of passengers and lessened the frequency of their trips. The long walk in sun along the long dusty road from the village, a first time experience, coupled with the extended wait for the untimely bus had exhausted him completely. He was dying to lie down in a comfortable place and rest for a while. A little way off, he saw a peepul tree with its crown of bushy branches welcoming him to come and ease his weary bones in its shade. He dragged himself to the place where the peepul tree stood unmindful of the fiery Sun, ready to shelter weary passers-by.

He sat on the ground on his haunches under the cool shade of the peepul tree, leaning his back against the trunk. Slowly, he stretched his legs. He felt as if he had suddenly been transported to Heaven from Hell. He stayed in that position for a while. It did not take long for drowsiness to overcome him.

A rustling movement, near him, woke him up. When he opened his eyes, he was surprised to see an old man sitting near him. Seeing him awake the old man asked, "Waiting for a bus?"

"Yes, I am going to Imphal."

"I also go to Imphal every month to withdraw my pension."

Maipak remained silent. The old man continued but this time, it was more of a comment to himself. With a long breath, he murmured slowly, "Imphal, a peaceful and lovely place once but turned into the graveyard of a battlefield now!"

He turned to Maipak and asked again, "Are you from Imphal?"

"Yes, I was born and grew up in Imphal. I live at Keishampat."

Without paying much attention to Maipak's reply, the old man took off his spectacles and wiped it with one end of his *pheijom*. He held it up with his wrinkled but nimble fingers to see whether the glasses were clear or not. Satisfied that they were clear, he put it on. The thick glasses made his narrow teary eyes, half covered with wrinkled folds of skin, look wide and sparkling. He forced a cough to clear his throat.

The old man spoke again. This time his voice was drowned in melancholy.

"I once worked in an office at Imphal. There was a time when I used to go to office riding on a bicycle covering a to and fro distance of 30 miles or so daily which the present day youngsters will find it hard to believe. It happened long ago."

The old man took a break to moisten his dry lips by licking with his tongue before he continued again in his toothless husky voice.

"In those days, I had nothing to fear. I could go anywhere at any time. Now, danger lurks everywhere. Anything can happen at any place at any given moment. No place is safe."

He took off his glasses and placed it on the ground near him. After wiping the sweat off his face with a white *khudei,* which he carried around hanging on his shoulder as a customary practice of men of his age, he leaned his head against the trunk of the peepul tree. He slowly closed his eyes as if keeping his eyes open caused him great physical exertion.

"Now, my strength has failed me. I find it difficult to move around but I still manage to go to Imphal by bus two or three times every month to withdraw my pension."

Maipak interrupted with a question, "Why do you go to Imphal many times every month, only to collect your pension?"

The old man continued, "Imphal Treasury Office is always crowded with pensioners like me. It is a great hurdle to get my pension book through the pension-counter. I have to wait for a long time after keeping my pension book at the counter with the usual fee neatly folded inside. It normally takes more than one or two days for my turn to come as I cannot reach there early."

"I never knew that one has to pay some sort of fee to withdraw pension and wait for such a long time."

"Once you visit Imphal Treasury Office you will see everything and come to know. The office is run almost entirely by women. The pension-counters are also staffed by women. You should not be deceived by their attractive painted faces. Behind the mask of make-up, there lies a sharp and biting tongue. If you forget to put your fee inside the pension book then you will hear the music of your lifetime, camouflaged by sweet but penetrating words. Your pension book will be stuck at the counter till you pay the fee. The men are no better. They are of the same stock. I pity that one day they themselves will become pensioners like me."

Suddenly, the old man got up and started arranging his *pheijom*.

"Oh, my forgetfulness! I sat down to take a short rest but I have prolonged it. I will be late for *lairik-taba*."

He was still arranging the folds of his *pheijom* and dusting it with the *khudei* when he said, "By the way, you said you are from Keishampat. Thourani-Indumukhi who sells *bora* at Keishampat Lairembi knows me very well. Whenever I go to Imphal I make it a point to buy *bora* from her and exchange greetings."

The old man was already on the move. In spite of his weak look he was very agile. He walked with very quick but smooth steps as if gliding in air. He shouted back, "If you happen to meet her, please tell her that Maimom Tomchou from Toubul has remembered her and covey my regards to her."

Maipak was now left alone. He had been sitting on the ground for a long time, in a posture very unusual to him. He lazily moved side to side to ease his body from numbness. Something on the ground reflected sunlight and hit his eyes directly. It was a pair of spectacles, the old man's glasses.

He picked it up and mused, "*The old man has left behind his spectacles. There is no chance for me to return the glasses to him. Anyway, I will take it with me and hand it over to Thourani-Indumukhi. She can give it to him when he comes to Imphal to withdraw his pension.*"

A bus soon came. Maipak got on the bus but it made many stops on the way to pick up passengers, delaying the short journey. He reached Keishampat in the evening. Thourani-Indumukhi was there at her place at the roadside. Of the many *bora-yonbis* at Keishampat, she was the most popular. When he approached her stall, she was frying a pan-full of mouth-watering *bora* to serve the endless line of her evening customers.

He edged his way close to her ignoring what the other customers would say and called her, "Thourani!"

Without looking up, she said, "Please wait for a while. Let me first serve those who have come before you."

"No, Thourani. I have not come to buy *bora*. I just wanted to hand you over something."

This time she looked up. "Oh! It's you Maipak. What's it?"

"Do you know one Maimom Tomchou from Toubul?"

"Oh yes, that old spectacled fellow. Whenever he came to Imphal, he made it a point to buy *bora* from me and pass sweet pleasantries. He was such a nice gentleman. It is a pity that he met his end in a very unfortunate circumstance."

"You mean he is dead?"

"Yes, he died last month."

Maipak got a sudden jolt and dropped the pair of spectacles in his hand. The glasses broke into splinters. He stood transfixed like a statue and glared at the broken pieces of glass.

She watched the broken spectacles and continued, "You must have read about the firing incident which took place at the bus parking near here, in the paper. Two motorcycle borne youths fired at another youth waiting for a bus. A stray bullet hit an old man as he got down from a bus, killing him at the spot. The old man was none other than Taibungo-Tomchou. He had come to Imphal to withdraw his monthly pension."

"I was the first one to identify his dead body. I remember vividly the way his body was lying on the ground in a sprawl, with his right hand still clutching his pension book. His smashed glasses, exactly like your broken spectacles, were lying nearby."

8

Your story

What is it that you're thinking? What is it that you want? What is it that you're doing? In such a busy thoroughfare with fast moving traffic why did you cross the road without looking to the left and the right? A speeding car nearly missed you by a hair's breadth. Were you after the girl who just drove off on a scooter? Oh, she! What a beauty! She is already out of sight. After all it was not only you, all those standing nearby also turned their heads to catch a glimpse of her.

You have been transferring rather gifting away your heart to any girl you see or meet on the road as if your heart were a dispersible object. It does not matter, nor do you care whether she knows and reciprocates your feelings or not. It is quite natural for someone like you in the prime of youth. Well, such flitting moments are the only times you can take out from your hectic schedule and enjoy yourself. You do not want to chase after a girl or waste time in pursuit of 'Love'. You can hardly afford to divert your attention from what you are doing.

You have to put in your best effort and work hard in the battle of survival if you want to live as an honest and free man. You know very well there is no one who will stand for you. All you have are your drunkard of a father, your sickly mother who toils day and night to keep the family from starving and your little sister. You do not have any well-to-do relative ready to lend a helping hand. What about your friends? It is a good question. Yes, you have many. But, it is because of them you left your house and came to Imphal.

You do not want to bluff and cheat people to earn money. You want only the hard earned money, 'sweat-money' so to say—enjoying the fruits of labour is what you treasure most. In your village, Maibam Lokpaching Chingmang, there is no place to work, nor is there any scope for doing business. The only possible business is what your mother is doing. She collects vegetables from the growers and sells them at Nambol market in the afternoon after traversing a long distance on foot. Khwairamband market, the main market at Imphal, is not that far away but since there is no mode of public transport from your village she has to walk a long distance to the main road to catch a bus to go there. It is easier and more convenient to sell the vegetables at Nambol.

Your friends and colleagues have been carried away by the 'winds of change' sweeping across the whole world—of course differing in nature, form, ideas and goals from one region to another. A change in the prevailing system is all they want. They do not care whether the change is for the better or worse. They had tried hard to influence you with their ideals to follow their footsteps. But you could never agree with and accept their biddings. They say something and do something else. They never care what they are doing is good, bad, beneficial or harmful to others— the question of right and wrong carries no meaning for them. They are ready to cheat, swindle or even use force for money. In short they are ready to do anything for money—they think and act only for it. But, you consider ill-gotten wealth is shameful, corrupting and inherently evil. If you argue with them about their unscrupulous leanings they say whatever they are doing is the right course of action. They consider you a fool. But you never care. How long could you stay in their midst—you had to leave your village to avoid their company. After passing Class XII you left your village for Imphal. You stayed in a rented room at Keishampat and tried to continue your studies at Imphal College. From your rented room you went to college to attend your classes riding on your old bicycle. Many of your classmates came to college on scooters and motorcycles. As soon as they reached college instead of attending classes they would cheer, roam and hang around corners as if they had come to attend some sort of entertainment programme. You stayed aloof from the fun-lovers. You might not be aware that some of the girl students had nicknamed you 'The Loner'.

Your mother's meagre earning from selling vegetables could hardly make ends meet. Now, she had to shoulder the additional burden of paying your room rent over and above your college fees. You had no alternative but to look out for part-time jobs. After college you started working as a private tutor for a small school boy, the youngest son of your landlord. That had taken care of the room rent. Your mother's health had also deteriorated; she found it difficult to carry on her business of selling vegetables at Nambol. To earn extra money to meet your family's expenses you started hawking door to door fancy goods whenever you were free.

However hard you tried to earn money to feed your family and continue your college you could never satisfy the needs. The wants kept mounting. How long could you go on with your study? No plausible solution was in sight except giving up your study and turning your full attention to earning.

Hawking fancy items and consumer goods had become your full time job. Even those who really did not need the goods were charmed by your innocent look, simple ways, impressive talks and polite manners—they could not resist from buying. You have an uncanny knack for selling goods. The sale was good. Your business picked up and you could save a little money in bank. You never wasted your time. In the evening when you were free you joined a computer course to learn how to handle and operate computers. You mastered the use and applications of Word and DTP software packages. Soon, you stopped hawking goods and joined a printing press. There you got chance to read many creative works while typesetting for printing. It tempted you to write and gave an irresistible urge to express your sentiments and feelings. You started dreaming of becoming a writer. You wrote:

Life, you embrace me tightly.
I do not know who you are; what is your relation with me.
A friend? A foe? What is that you want from me?
It is immaterial whether you are a friend or a foe.
I can never leave you even for a moment.
But you are trying to leave me behind.
Where do you want to go? Where do you want to live?
Whether you love me or not, I can't help but worry about you.

Once you started writing you simply could not give up. Writing gave you peace of mind and you found happiness and solace in it. You wrote many poems but did not have the heart to show them to your colleagues. At long last you selected two poems and sent them to Imphal Free Press. After that every Sunday you opened the literary column of the paper to see your poems in print. But, your poems never appeared. Nevertheless it did not deter you from writing. You continued to write.

Once in a while you went to your house to meet your parents and sister. Your mother and sister were jubilant to see you. Your father was his usual self—he was still drowning himself in drinks without caring for the family. Your mother was very worried about your little sister. She was no longer a small girl. A charming lass, surrounded by rowdy boys of the neighbourhood—what might become of her? You too were worried about her. Since you were a man you could leave your village and come to Imphal whenever you wanted. But your sister could not do so since she was a girl. Most of the young men of your village were not restrained and disciplined. You were afraid they might tease and disturb your sister. Even in your dream you saw the boys teasing her on her way to school. You pondered over the problems of your family and thought of bringing all of them to Imphal. It was not an easy thing to do. With your meagre earning how could you manage to keep them at Imphal? You were in a dilemma.

When you last visited your family you had heard, "Tomchou's son has been appointed as a police constable. They seem to have spent a lot for it. They have disposed of all their landed properties." You know Tomchou's son very well—a crook. They live four houses away from yours, toward the east. Your mother's words keep ringing in your ears, "It is said to be a very paying job—they would be able to buy back everything in no time." In this land tainted with extortion, corruption and nepotism where kidnapping and killing have become the order of the day there is no place for a modest person like you. Only a handpicked few have amassed enormous wealth and consolidated their positions by means which will put even Devil to shame.

Today is Saturday, a new moon day. Though it is just after dusk, the winding lane is already engulfed in complete darkness since electric supply has failed. It is not very far from the press where you work. You are returning after work with an old Manipuri film song on your lips—*Pun-shi ngak-e-ko nang-se . . . khang-de-ko nang-se* (Life, you are strange . . . you are a perplexing one). No one is out on the lane. A little way off, the building where you are staying is faintly visible. Flickering lights of candles can be seen through the windows of some of the rooms. On reaching the gate when you are about to turn in, someone standing in a dark corner shouts aloud, "Halt." You get a severe jolt. Hair on your head bristles. You abruptly stop singing.

"Raise your hands."

You reluctantly lift up your hands in fright. Someone in plain clothes comes out and feels around all over your body with his hands.

"He has got it, Sir."

You suddenly remember. Five thousand rupees you took out from your account in bank thinking, "Tomorrow is Sunday. I will go home and give some money to mother for buying paddy this harvest season," is in your pocket.

"Get in the car without a sound," orders the person.

You think of shouting but it will be of no use. Who will come to help you at such a time? When you look around you see a white car parked a little way off. Another person sitting inside the car opens the back door and rushes out. Two of them drag you and push you inside the car. Each of them sits at your sides and you are forced to sit in the middle. A third person is already sitting in the front seat along with the driver. As soon as the back door is closed the car drives out. No one has seen you being kidnapped. Inside the car you are made to bend over your head. You cannot make out toward which direction the car is heading. After driving for a while they tie your hands behind your back and blindfold you with a piece of black cloth.

After some time they park the car. The person sitting in front speaks to you referring your name and surname precisely. You are aghast. You ponder, "Are they policemen in plainclothes? Or, members of which organisation? How come, they know my name and surname? Why have they kidnapped me?"

He calls you again. You remain silent. One of the persons sitting at your side says, "Should I bash him, Sir? He does not answer even when you call him by his name."

The person sitting in front continues, "We have all the information. For which organisation are you collecting money?"

You cannot fathom their intention, nor can you answer the question. Your mother's words, "It is said to be a very paying job—they would be able to buy back everything in no time," keep coming back.

They leave you behind and drive away the car.

It is a long time since local newspapers have stopped to bring out their publications out of compulsion. No one has heard about your disappearance. However, news broadcast by AIR, Imphal has mentioned something about you—a bullet riddled un-identified dead body was recovered from a place near Iroisemba Zoo. At your house your mother and sister are waiting for you to bring money to buy paddy this harvest season.

9

Abok Macha, our Small Granny

I t was the day I reached home after staying away for more than four years. Not knowing what to do, I went for a leisurely walk after dinner. Vast paddy fields spread out in front of me; distant dark hills encircling the valley; shadowy bamboo groves in the distance—all looked enchanting in the moonlit night. Why shouldn't it be a beholding sight? At the city crowded till late in the night, with high-rise buildings on both sides of roads, where glaring artificial lights had chased away darkness, moonlight had shied away from the manmade lights. No one bothered about the moon or seemed to be aware of its presence. Back at our lonely small village, I felt uneasiness at the pleasant contrast. It was too early to go to bed and I had nothing to do. Dragging myself slowly, I reached the crossing where the dusty road leading to our village with ruts made by the wheels of bullock-carts branched off from the main road. The majestic peepul tree was still standing in full regal splendour at its place at the roadside corner.

Suddenly, I remembered Abok Macha, who once had a stall at the foot of the peepul tree. People used to call her Ene-Binashakhi but to us, children of the village, she was simply Abok Macha, our small granny. She was small in stature and foul-mouthed but generous and kind-hearted. A small hut built at the foot of the tree served as her stall. Every afternoon she sat there to sell her home-made munchies. She did a brisk business by the village standard. She had no close relative of her own and lived alone. But she was very fond of me and treated me as her own grandson—I don't know why. Every day when I returned from school, she would call me and offer sweets to eat. Because of it, my friends teased and called me 'Abok Macha's grandson'. Annoyed, I tried to avoid her many a time. But, I was not always successful.

During the rainy season when cloudbursts were frequent, on my way back home from school I often had to take shelter in her stall to escape from the watery onslaught. She never wasted such an opportunity to tell me stories. She had a knack for telling stories. One particular story, the story of Chinglai, the fire-breathing dragon and Nachal, a petite millipede was my favourite. She told me the same story many times but each time she cleverly presented it in a different way so that it remained an evergreen story. I never got tired of hearing it again and again.

Chinglai was the king of all the animals living in forests over the ranges of hills and mountains spread out in all directions. He lived in caves, changing from one cave to another according to season as he wished. He also changed his form quite often to suit his mood. He breathed out fire when he was disturbed and annoyed. When he snored the rumble could be heard far and wide, and all the animals shook with fright. When he rolled inside the caves the surrounding hills shivered causing landslides that swept away villages and blocked roads.

Abok Macha said, "Mind you, there is much difference between the shivering of the hills and earthquake. Only those who had experienced both personally can tell the difference."

Chinglai was a good and just ruler surrounded by old and wise ministers and advisors. He was untainted by greed, lust and anger, though he himself was not aware of the damages caused by his snoring and rolling while sleeping. As long as his old and wise ministers and advisors were alive they managed to keep his snoring and rolling in sleep under control. This they did by making him sleep on his belly on the floor of caves specially prepared by spreading layers after layers of fine golden sand. But, the old and wise ministers and advisors died one by one in old age. Young ministers and advisors who came in their place were inexperienced but very greedy. They saw that they could gain more power and riches by intimidating the poor subjects and making them suffer more—a totalitarian regime. They used unsuspecting Chinglai as a means to achieve their sinister designs. They made him sleep in supine position on the hard rocky floor saying that it would be good for his backbones. That did the trick. Chinglai snored loudly and rolled frequently in sleep, thereby causing untold damages to lives and properties.

Nachal who lived not very far away from the cave where Chinglai was presently residing had had the misfortune of being carried away in landslides almost every night. He always came back unscathed as he could roll tightly into a hard and tough ball. But, he lost everything he owned.

An infuriated Nachal decided to punish the wrongdoers and put an end to the atrocities perpetrated by them. He lay in wait at the mouth of the cave. When the sun rose above the hills, Chinglai came out with his retinue of young ministers and advisors for their routine inspection of the surrounding forests. Nachal saw his opportunity. Before anyone could stop him he rolled tightly into a ball and rolled down the side of the cave fast and landed on Chinglai's soft belly. He bit his belly button hard with all his might. Unable to withstand the sudden excruciating pain Chinglai swayed his head from side to side and blew out powerful flames through his nostrils. The flames licked the ministers and advisors around him unaware. With their furs on fire, they frightened out of their wits ran away, never to return again.

Abok Macha said, "A petite Nachal had the courage to challenge and fight the powerful wrongdoers. You should never lose courage whatever happens to you." In another version, Nachal did not lay in wait but threw an open challenge to Chinglai and his retinue of ministers and advisors. Yet in one more version Nachal complained to Chinglai against his ministers and advisors. Chinglai investigated, verified and confirmed the misdeeds of his ministers and advisors. Blowing out fire through his nostrils, an angry Chinglai chased the culprits away.

"Shashi, have you returned from school? Come here for a while."

I had tried to sneak away without being seen. But, Abok Macha had seen me. Pretending not to hear her, I kept on walking.

"You, insolent boy! I lovingly called you but you go on walking as if you haven't heard me. Come and have *Boroi Heingan*."

At the very mention of *Boroi Heingan*, I had forgotten everything about my friends' teasing. I ran towards her. She gave me *Boroi Heingan*, wrapped in a piece of banana-leave. Without a word, I took it and ran home straight lest my friends would see me.

"You, naughty boy! Can't you sit and eat properly. If you eat while running you'll smear yourself and spoil your dress," Abok Macha shouted at the top of her voice. I did not pay attention to what she was saying for my mind was already occupied with other thoughts.

I was panting when I ran past our gate and reached the courtyard. Mother was pounding rice in the northern outhouse. She inquired, "Why have you come running so fast?"

I halted near the Tulsi, sacred basil plant, planted in the centre of the courtyard.

"Nothing doing," I replied half out of breath.

Mother stopped pounding rice, placed the wooden pestle leaning on the wooden mortar and came near me.

"If it's nothing then why did you come running so fast?" There was a note of alarm in her voice. I kept standing.

"What's that in your hand?"

"*Boroi Heingan* given by Abok Macha."

Even before I could complete the sentence, she snatched it from me and threw it away. She pulled my hair at the back of my head and boxed my ear, all the while reprimanding me.

"You have become very naughty. Why did you accept anything to eat given by that evil woman who has done away with everyone near and dear to her. She is a witch. Let your father return, I'll get you punished."

When *Paba* returned home, mother told him everything but he did not take the matter seriously. She was angry at his indifference. Pouting her lips, she said, "Well, well . . . she'll put your son also under her evil spell . . . that witch of a woman."

Paba could no longer remain silent. "Shashi, obey your mother. Never accept anything offered by Ene-Binashakhi in future."

After that day I stopped taking anything offered by Abok Macha so lovingly. But, that did not deter her from calling me to her stall. I told her I had indigestion, my stomach was upset, etc. However tempting the sweets and munchies were I did not take anything, pretending not to be feeling well.

When I was studying in Class X, a severe draught struck. Cracks developed in our paddy field and the paddy plants wilted; not even a single grain of rice was collected. Every household in the village had to undergo a lot of hardships because of the scarcity of water. People had to walk a long distance to fetch water from an almost dried up brook. When our paddy field, the only source of our family's income, produced nothing both my parents had to run hither and thither to save us from starvation. In our small village, there was no place to work. Every day they used to get up early in the morning to go to Imphal and work there as daily wage labourers but what they earned was hardly enough even for two square meals a day. It was at that time, I had to pay my fees for appearing in the High School Leaving Certificate (HSLC) Examination. But, where was the money to pay the fees when we did not have even to buy food? All the households in our village were poor families like ours; there was none who could offer money on loan. I felt like crying—shall I give up my study without appearing in the HSLC Examination at all? At such a time when everyone was suffering untold miseries, Abok Macha came to our house one early morning. As soon as she entered our gate, she started calling out loudly.

"Hi . . . Shashi, hi . . . Shashi, is your father in?"

I heard mother murmuring inside the house, "This evil woman, why has she come at such a time when we are about to go out to earn our daily bread? The very sight of her will spoil our day."

"Yes, he is in." There was a slight tinge of hatred in her voice.

Paba was alarmed. He ran out.

"*Ene*, what brings you here?"

"What I've heard . . . is it true? People are saying . . . Shashi will give up his study because of your inability to pay his examination fees."

Paba replied dejectedly, "I've no means."

Abok Macha came forward slowly and sat on the edge of the raised veranda, with her legs dangling. She untied a knot in her *enaphi* and took out a bundle of currency notes. I had no idea of the total amount.

"Take it. See if it is enough for Shashi's fees. If not, I'll give you more."

Paba could not take the money. He was dumbfounded.

"You need not return it. I am paying it for Shashi . . . my grandson."

Paba did not move. He kept standing like a statue. Mother went out and took the money.

"Thank you, *Ene*."

I could see and hear everything from my room through the window. At that moment my happiness knew no bounds. Now, I am able to stand on my feet only because of Abok Macha's generosity. Unable to see the people of our village suffering untold hardships due to the scarcity of water, that very year she donated land and paid for digging the public tank from which everyone in our village is enjoying water.

I slowly moved closer to the peepul tree. No trace was left of Abok Macha's stall. With a heavy heart, I turned for home. In the distant swampy areas at the foothills, *Lanmei Thanbis* could be seen to be prancing around. In my childhood days whenever we saw *Lanmei Thanbi*, we, shivering with fright, used to run home shouting, "*Lanmei Thanbi toi toi. Hangen poura kit.*" People say, "*Lanmei Thanbis,* flickering in the distance, are the departed souls playing merrily."

I couldn't help but wonder, "Is Abok Macha's soul among them?"

10

Loneliness

Nightly silence came creeping over the parched paddy fields, cracked with thirst for the seasonal rain. Perched on a branch of the bushy canopy of a mango tree, a nightly owl hooted idly in the distance, after waking up from a deep slumber and broke the silence. It spread its wings wide and flapped vigorously to get ready for the nocturnal hunt.

To the ailing Earth with its protective plant cover skinned by the humans to expose the raw soil, now unable to trap water and retain moisture, the life-giving Sun had become a destroyer. Night had brought a welcome change. It had undone the ghastly acts of the summer Sun trying to scorch everything it set its rays on, both living and non-living alike. The silvery moonlight had concealed the raw wounded skin of the Earth. The temperature had come down to a bearable level if not comfortable.

The cool refreshing air of the night invited a field mouse to come out of its burrow. It poked its head, looked to the left and right to survey the surroundings for any threat to its life. After making sure that no danger lurked around, it stealthily ran out in search of food. The light was poor and the colour of the hair covering its tiny body matched that of the ground, a perfect camouflage but it had failed to deceive the sharp eyes of the owl. The jerky movement of the mouse gave itself away. The owl swooped down swiftly without the slightest sound and caught the mouse in its sharp claws. Up it flew carrying the mouse tightly clasped in its claws—the first and final flight for the poor helpless mouse. The claws tightened. The mouse squeaked in agony before its life ran out, a feeble squeak only to be drowned in the nightly silence.

Nightly silence reigned supreme. No sound came from Sanatomba's isolated but usually noisy mud-plastered bamboo and reed hut of a house, standing at the foothills. In his effort to buy a government job, he had squandered all he owned to grease the palms of the greedy public leaders who hoodwinked him with their sweet talks and false promises. He was completely broke. In the battle of survival, he had no alternative left but to settle at the desolate place and try his hands at growing vegetables to feed his family of four; he, his wife, a son and a daughter.

The long awaited rain-bearing monsoon clouds had failed to appear, making the air hot and dry. All the nearby tanks, ponds, canals and streams had dried up. Not even a single drop of water was left. A severe draught had struck. The strong sun combined with the parched air had wilted all the plants and vegetables in his garden. There was no hope of reviving it. They had to walk a long distance to fetch their daily requirement of water from an almost dried up brook. The trickle flow of water, their only source, would not last more than a week at most.

Both the husband and wife sat together to discuss the situation and their problems but no solution was in sight without the elusive rain. After deliberation at length, it was decided that she would go to her parental house, a floating hut built on *phumdi* in the Loktak Lake with their two ever-busy hectic children. He would stay back to guard the house as long as there was water in the dying brook and wait for the rain.

He was left alone in the lonesome house; a lonely man with no soul miles around. The house, once a lively one, filled with the gaiety of his children prancing around and sharing pranks was now very lonely without the slightest sound. The children had taken along their noise that he once thought was deafening.

The night was still young. He, an early sleeper, went to bed but could not close his eyes even for a wink. When his children were around, he longed for silence so that he could rest for a while in peace but he had never imagined the nightly silence would be so disturbing. He rolled on the bed from side to side, listening to the sound of silence. *The sound of silence? Only experience can tell.*

Unable to sleep, he sat up. The roar of the nightly silence became louder and louder in his ears. Above the noise, he heard the voices of his children. His son was complaining against his daughter, "*Paba*, please come and see what *Cheche* has done."

"*Paba,* I've done nothing."

"She's lying. She is a very mischievous girl. She has spilled water all over the place so that I'll slip when I walk."

"I didn't do it intentionally. I kicked the bucket by mistake and spilled the water."

"No, *Paba*. She is lying again. I saw her deliberately kicking the bucket. She always has fun at my cost."

"No, no. He's the one who is lying. He's trying to get me punished."

Fed up with the children's noisy quarrel, Sanatomba shouted at them, "Will you two keep quiet for a while!"

He suddenly realised; he was alone and shouting in the dark. The imposed loneliness was playing tricks on him. His shout had quietened the noise of the nightly silence ringing in his ears. He felt a great relief and wiped the sweat off his forehead with a piece of cloth. Feeling better he laid down and tried to sleep.

He heard his wife calling from the kitchen, "Dinner is served. Please wash your hands and bring the children along."

Like corn popping in a popcorn machine, his wife continued to rapid-fire a volley of verbal pellets, "Please don't waste water. I had to walk a long distance in the sun and waste the whole day to fetch water. You wouldn't care to help me. I have to toil like a slave to run the family but you never count my labour . . ."

". . . I never had to work like this when I was with my parents. Everything was available at hand. There was no dearth of anything. Even in my wildest dream I could never imagine that one day I would be walking such a long distance only to fetch water, leave aside other household chores . . ."

". . . So much for your promise to treat me like the proverbial queen, I've been fooled by your sweet nonsense. You'll come to know of my importance only when I'm gone . . ."

Sanatomba could not remain silent any longer. In his husky and breathy voice, he said, "Okay, can't you shut your mouth for a while? I've had enough of your lecture. Tomorrow, I'll go to fetch water."

"Tee . . . hee . . . hee . . . ," his wife laughed sarcastically and mockingly said, "You will fetch water!"

Sanatomba opened his eyes slowly only to find that he had been sleeping alone in the dark and dreaming. His wife's nagging, which he hated but endured as there was no escape, was now music to his ears.

This loneliness is killing me. The nightly silence is really frightening.

It is making me hear voices, the noise of silence.

The loud frightening noise of the nightly silence has deafened me.

No, I must be wrong. How can silence make noise when it means cessation of sound? I am imagining things. I have gone out of my head.

This unusual nightly silence in loneliness is beyond my tolerance. First thing I will do tomorrow is pack my belongings, leave this place and head for my in-laws' house.

He felt around in the dark and found what he was looking for, a match box. He struck a matchstick. The room was lighted in the faint glow of the burning matchstick. The tiny flame quickly flickered out. He got down, struck another matchstick and headed for the front door.

He slowly opened the door and came out. Outside, it was totally dark. Cool and refreshing breeze was gently blowing. As he got down from the veranda, a big drop of rain landed on his nose—a welcome signal. He looked up only to be blinded by a flash of lightning. The rumbling noise of thunder followed. Soon, it started raining heavily.

A jubilant Sanatomba stood in the rain. An earthy smell brought forth by the parched earth quenching its thirst struck his nose. The rain had washed away all his worries. He had forgotten his loneliness. Softly humming a song, he went inside the house.

First thing I will do tomorrow is go to my in-laws' house and bring my wife and children home.

11

Recharge Card

Holiday plan, I have never made before for I am not obsessed with travelling to faraway places that requires elaborate planning. Nor am I fascinated by new faces—unknown companies and strange places irk me. I easily get bored with my friends' stories of the new places they have visited during their vacations. The photographs they brought back fail to fascinate me. I would rather spend my holidays alone, nearer home, doing odd things that I have not been able to do during the hectic workdays or visiting the tourist spots nearby to watch the holidaymakers gathered there from a distance. Why waste time and money when there are so many things to do, so many places to visit nearer home?

A lonely person, I am, I wish to be left alone most of the time. May be it is related to my Polynesian origin. I have a strange feeling I am the odd one out when I am amidst my fellow countrymen. It has nothing to do with racial discrimination, for I have never experienced anyone treating me differently. Nevertheless, I feel that my looks are quite different and people always stare at me wherever I go. A complex born out of the colour of my skin—may be it's only that. Once, I told one of my friends about my feeling of uneasiness whenever people look at me.

Pat came the reply, "Just ignore them and do what you are doing. Do you think people don't look at me? I don't pay any attention to them as long as they don't disturb me."

But, my visit to the Barbican Centre last spring has completely changed my outlook. It had tickled my mind and instilled an insatiable urge in me to visit a secluded place in the north east corner of India. I was left completely devastated. The only way to compose myself was to visit this numinous land. Well, the Barbican Centre lies close to my place at the heart of 140,000 square metre residential estates in London, known as the Barbican. After the area was completely razed to ground during the Second World War, the Barbican was built as 'the City's gift to the Nation' by the Corporation of London. Now, it can proudly claim as the largest cultural complex in Europe. The Barbican has become one of the most important promoters of international theatre in Britain through BITE programme. BITE stands for Barbican International Theatre Events.

During my visit there, I got an opportunity to witness a performance, an allegorical poem of a play, by a theatrical group from a petite nondescript state of the Indian union. It is the performance that had captivated and propelled me to visit the place, my dream place, a mystical land comprising of nine concentric ranges of hills encircling a valley, an erstwhile paradise. But, unfortunate turn of events through the passage of time has deprived it much of its glory.

Culture and traditions show the identity of a group of people and bind them together. Where do people stand when their cultural traditions are lost? This question kept pestering and made me restless. It is amazing how such a small group of people are trying to protect and preserve their cultural traditions, much against the odds—amidst genocide, political instability, venality, unemployment, extortion and misuse of power and money. The natives are pleading the Wise Men to come forward to protect and save them from their miseries. Who are the Wise Men? Why have they gone into hiding? What is the ideology of the numerous ethnic groups inhabiting the place that keeps and binds them together all these years? What are the forces threatening and trying to break up the oneness of the peoples? Certainly they are looking for answers to numerous questions that are troubling them and pragmatic solutions to their problems. Strangely, many of the actors resembled Polynesians to a great extent and they reminded me of my roots. I must visit the place to quench my thirst to know more about the place and satisfy my curiosity—a decision I made then and there after watching the play.

I made my plan to visit the place a secret and searched the web to learn more about it. Many websites devoted to attract tourists are there— nature's bounty, evergreen forests, a beautiful valley surrounded by bluish hills, a large fresh water lake where brow-antlered deer dance in the only floating wildlife sanctuary in the world. The more I learned about the place, the greater was the pull towards it, a place where festivals lasted twelve months a year, so pure and unspoilt by the modern mechanical world. It had kept me spellbound, *"Ah, it is the place I have been waiting so long to visit! No, no other place for me but only this place of my dreams!"* With this firm conviction I applied for visa to visit India and obtained it without any problem.

One fine day in August, I landed at Delhi after midnight. I halted there for one day and caught a flight to Imphal. When the announcement for landing at Imphal Airport came I was thrilled, *"In a few moments I will be united with my dream place!"* The plane slowly circled over the valley encircled by bluish hills. Through the window I saw the entire valley segmented into small green squares reaching far out to the hills, unmistakably rice fields that I had seen in photographs in internet. I gasped in delight, *"Oh, what a lovely sight, I am blessed!"*

After landing at the airport, I walked to the reporting counter for foreigners. Oh lo! I made a great mistake. With my looks closely resembling the natives, no one would have questioned me had I gone without reporting. But since I had reported there, I was asked to produce PAP—it stands for Protected Area Permit. I had never heard of it before. I was informed, "Without PAP no foreigner is permitted to enter Manipur." I was detained at the Airport for entering Manipur without valid papers. They would not listen to my earnest pleas and I was sent back to Delhi on the same aircraft I had come. But, I was not deterred. I took a solemn vow, *"I will not visit any other place in India before I set my feet on the soil of Manipur."*

On my arrival back in Delhi after being deported from Imphal, I purchased a book from the airport to pass my time and learn more of Indian culture. The book, 'the Indian Epics Retold' by R.K. Narayan, published by Penguin Books India Pvt. Ltd., a compilation of three earlier volumes, 'the Ramayana', 'the Mahabharata' and 'Gods, Demons, and Others' turned out to be quite interesting. I was introduced to many characters and stories from Indian Mythology that I had never heard before.

In Delhi I obtained a copy of the application form for PAP. There again I had trouble in filling the form. I was to fill in the 'Purpose of my visit', 'Likely duration of visit', 'Arrangements for travel & accommodation that have been made', 'Places proposed to visit' and many other information which I had not come prepared. I had come with an open mind to go wherever I wanted and visit as many places as I could. I did not know much about the places worth to see in Manipur. Anyway, I entered all the places I had seen in the websites. It took me five weekdays of running from one table to another in the office of the Ministry of Home Affairs to get my PAP. I also paid double the amount of fee as I had not applied at least four weeks before the visit.

Exactly seven days later, armed with PAP I took a flight to Imphal again. This time I was allowed to stay back after answering a lot of queries, which I was told was necessary for security reasons. I left for the city in a taxi. The ride from the airport was thrilling in the sense that I got to learn a lot and see many new things that could never be dreamt of anywhere else. The roads were full of portholes, here and there garbage heaps dotted with colourful plastic bits were piled up beside the roads, lending beauty to the surroundings—a truly exciting experience. After a short enjoyable bumpy ride, I checked in a hotel where the driver took me. The hotel was located in a crowded part of the city.

I rested for a while. When I came out of my room after washing and changing into a new dress, it was already five in the evening. I went to the reception counter to inquire about the interesting places where I could go and spend the evening. Two persons from the Home Department were waiting for me there. They introduced themselves and informed me that they were assigned to check on me and keep track of my movements so that I did not go to troublesome and unsafe places, and land myself into trouble. I could not help but wonder, *"So they have been shadowing me. How wonderful, they take so much personal care for each and every foreigner!"* They advised me not to move out of Imphal. If at all I was to leave Imphal then I must inform them. Meeting them had made me forget the very purpose of coming to the reception counter. I slowly came out of the hotel and walked aimlessly for a while. I looked behind my shoulders to see if the two persons from the Home Department were still following me or not. Much to my relief, they could not be seen anywhere.

I continued walking and came to a market run by women. It must be the famous women's market of Imphal I had heard about. All the vendors were women. Most of the buyers also were women. The road outside the market was ankle deep in mud. Unmindful of the mud and garbage heaps piled up nearby, on drier ground at the roadside many women were selling vegetables. Inside the market on rows of raised platforms, covered with corrugated iron sheets to shelter from sun and rain, women were selling everything from vegetables and fishes to clothes and cosmetics. *"A rare sight! Where on earth can one find such a place?"*

I spent around one hour there. Many of the women looked like my mother and grandmother. I was completely at ease, I felt as if I was with my own people. No one bothered to look at me. My uneasy feeling of people staring at me back home in London was gone.

Once in a while, some of the vendors beckoned me and said something in their native tongue, of which I had no idea. Probably they were calling me in to buy what they were selling. I simply shook my head. I did not open my mouth at all lest they would come to know of my ignorance of their language and my foreigner status. Soon, they started packing up. I had no idea, the market closed so early. I decided to come the next day with a guide and bring my camera. I left the market and went back to my hotel.

Next day, I woke up early and got ready for roaming around Imphal. Someone knocked on the door. I looked at my watch adjusted to the local time. It was exactly 8 a.m. I suddenly remembered that it must my guide. I had requested the receptionist to arrange for a guide to show me around the nearby market and send him to my room at 8 a.m. I mused, *"How prompt people here are!"*

I opened the door. Outside, someone in a dress I had never seen before was standing. A strange luminous brilliance reflected from him dazzled my eyes and I was awestruck. On his head was a gilded crown. He was holding a golden mace in his right hand. He said, "Good morning, I'm Yama Dharma, your guide."

I could not help but admire his impressive costume, *"How nice of the receptionist! He has sent a guide donned up nicely in the local costume to impress me."*

I said, "Good morning. Please do come in. I'll ready in a minute."

He refused to come inside and said he would wait outside. Still half-confused, I repeated, "I'll be ready in a minute."

I hurriedly put on my sneakers, got hold of a small bag containing my camera, came out and locked the room. My guide was standing a little way off with his legs crossed and hands leaning on the mace. As soon as he saw me coming, he started walking towards the lift. I silently followed him and we went downstairs. The receptionist was looking up at the hotel's register. He did not see us coming out of the lift. The lobby was deserted. I hesitated a moment, *"Should I leave the key to the room?"* I thought it did not matter since I would not go far. We sneaked out without being seen.

After walking a few steps, I saw two shops, not very far away. People were standing in a long line before the first shop. However, there was no one in front of the second shop. Someone standing before the second shop was waving a sheaf of cards and shouting, "Buy one at half the price and get three free," to attract customers

I asked my guide, "What are the shops selling? One is so crowded while the other cannot attract even a single customer."

"They are selling recharge cards."

"For cell phone?"

Waiting for an answer from my guide, I kept watching the shops intently. Just then, a flagged car escorted by armoured cars sped in. Someone, possibly a political heavyweight, got down from the flagged car and bought big stacks of cards from the second shop and left hurriedly.

After a brief pause, my guide replied, "Those shops are selling recharge cards for life."

His answer baffled me. "Recharge cards for life?"

"Oh, you are new here. So you won't be able to understand the things around here."

We stood in a corner while he explained, "In Manipur everyone needs to recharge their lives once in a while to stay alive. The two shops are selling different categories of recharge cards. The crowded shop is selling recharge cards for common people who honestly work hard to earn their livelihood and live hand to mouth, while the other shop is selling recharge cards for public leaders, bureaucrats and higher echelons who churn the society and relish the cream."

I said, "So that explains for the crowd at the first shop. It is a pity everywhere in the world it is the privileged class who gets the first and better choice. Here also it is the same. They even have separate shops specially reserved for them."

My guide said, "Here it's not that. Our system is different. Here public leaders are not public leaders, bureaucrats are not bureaucrats, and higher echelons are not higher echelons as you understand."

He then spoke at length to explain that the recharge cards for common hardworking people were very costly, still there was no dearth of buyers as everyone wanted to stay alive. The recharge cards for the influential group were dirt cheap. They could buy as many cards as they wanted at a throwaway price. His explanation did not make any sense to me. I could not see any valid reason for keeping the price of the recharge cards for the poor common people high while that of the affluent ones was kept so low.

I enquired, "Why is it so? Who controls the price of the cards?"

His face broke into a mischievous smile and said, "You have to learn the Scripture. Only then you will be able to understand."

I got more perplexed, "I can't make head or tail of what you're saying."

Sensing the difficulty I was having in following his words, he said, "Brahma regulates the price of the recharge cards on the advice of the Supreme Commander."

"But, who is Brahma?"

"Brahma is the creator. At the moment there is shortage of accommodation in Heaven. So He is trying to regulate the flow of people coming to Heaven. A new residential complex is coming up to accommodate all the hardworking and honest people. Once the complex is ready the price of the recharge cards will soar up. It will be astronomically high. Then all the common hardworking and honest people will be compelled to leave this place and come to Heaven."

What he was saying seemed like a big joke to me—recharge cards for life, scripture, Creator, Supreme Commander, Heaven, etc. so mystifying, it was like a fairy tale. I had a feeling that my guide was an eccentric trying his way out to earn my respect.

Still for the sake of continuing our talk and keeping him occupied, I said, "What about the elite group, the cream of the society?"

"Oh, they? They are barred from coming to Heaven. Brahma is trying to keep them back here. If they come, they will pollute Heaven like they are doing here. Once they set their feet there, Heaven will no longer be Heaven. Their tall talks and false promises will spoil the sanctity of Heaven. It is the reason why the price of their recharge cards is kept as low as possible."

At this point, his talk became more interesting. I said, "When will the residential complex be ready?"

"It will be ready within the blinking of Brahma's eyes."

"So soon!"

"Yes, to us, celestial beings, it is what you call 'a fraction of a second'. But, converted to your measurement of time, it is thousands of years. It takes an eon for Brahma to complete blinking his eyes once."

The talk became more appealing. I said, "An eon is not a specific measurement."

He replied, "You're right. Say, an eon is equivalent to four thousand years of your time. The residential complex will be ready in four thousand years."

"So, it's still a long time before the construction of the residential complex is completed."

"No, the residential complex is almost ready. We are at the vague end of the period of four thousand years.

"I could not help but ask him another question, "What will happen to the elite group?"

"Since there is no place for them in Heaven, they will remain here doing what they love and have been doing so long. They will continue to live here as cicadas, houseflies, mosquitoes and leeches, and go on flying all over the places, chirping, buzzing, yelling, grunting and sucking blood of other animals to their hearts' content."

I stared at him in astonishment, "*An eccentric in a funny costume who considered himself to be a celestial being or am I imagining things?*" My thought ran wild.

Boom! The building shook and threw me off balance. I dropped the book in my hand. I suddenly realised I had been reading, and slowly slipped into reverie—the characters in the book had come alive. Everything came back to me and my mind became clear, now. I had got up early and was reading the morning's paper while eagerly waiting for the guide I had asked for to turn up. The headline said forty eight hours' general strike had been called by some social organisations in protest against the arresting and killing of a man claimed to be innocent. 'General Strike'—what could it mean? I was confused. I lifted the intercom and dialled the number of the receptionist to enquire about it. I was told, it meant all the shops and market would be closed, no vehicle would ply on the roads, no one would come out of their houses—a complete standstill of life. I had to cancel all my programmes and stay inside my room the whole day. To pass my time I had opened R.K. Narayan's 'the Indian Epics Retold' and started reading again the stories I had already read.

A bomb exploded at the nearby market. Police cordoned the area. The whole day I remained inside my room. In the evening, the two persons from the Home Department came to my room and informed me to leave Imphal as early as possible as the situation had gone from bad to worse. I argued that I had permission to stay in Manipur for one week. But they would not listen. Much to my displeasure, the hotel's management arranged to cancel my return ticket and buy another ticket to Delhi for the next day.

The next day, I left for airport in a vehicle provided by the Home Department. My visit to Manipur had come to an abrupt end but my mind was still with the people of Manipur.

"O Manipur! The land of my dreams, you can't hide and run away from me. I would come again and play in your lap during my next vacation."

12

Mauled Cub

Tombi's mother opened the back door to let them go, stood for a while watching them leave and heaved a sigh of relief. A heavy load had suddenly been removed from her head. She thought of waking up Tombi but decided not to, "Let her sleep a little while longer. It's still very early."

She quickly finished her morning chores and opened the door of her store. Customers were already lined up outside. She changed her mind and called out loudly.

"Tombi . . . Tombi . . ."

Tombi's preoccupied mind was too busy to hear her mother's call. After calling three or four times, she stopped lest people would take her to be an obstreperous woman and went on attending to the customers.

A bus pulled up. Many passengers alighted from the bus and poured into the shop. Now, the customers were far too many for her to handle alone.

She shouted again, "Tombi . . . Tombi . . . Do you hear me?"

This time, Tombi got up with a start. "Yes, Mama. What's it?"

"Can you come and help me for a moment?"

Tombi went down, opened the connecting door and entered the small crammed shop, panting. She seemed to have lost all her energy but forced herself to help the customers to get what they wanted while her mother collected money.

Their shop stocked with varieties of items from all sorts of soft drinks to fresh fruits, cosmetics to boot polish, spices to dry fish, even stationery items, and thread and needle except readymade garments attracted more customers than the other shops in the row. It occupied a ground floor room of their house, a two storeyed wooden building with mud plastered reed walls, built next to the road at Moirang Crossing, a stopover for the buses plying on Imphal-Churachandpur highway. Needless to say, it was not only the items neatly displayed in front of the shop but also the warm smile her mother wore permanently on her face that lured the customers.

The bus honked repeatedly. The last customer ran off after collecting change from her mother.

Noticing her off-colour face her mother inquired, "You look so pale. What happened?"

Tombi wanted to tell her so many things but could not decide where to start. The whole morning she had been lost in her thought, wondering whether she should disclose. They had already suffered so much. She was afraid any disturbing news might put her mother in a state of delirium.

She lied, "Nothing . . . just exhausted."

One more bus came and stopped nearby. Their shop started swelling with the passengers trying to buy what they wanted during the short stopover.

Her mother turned to her and said, "If you aren't feeling well, go and take rest. I can handle the customers alone."

Tombi cautiously got up, sluggishly went through the connecting door and dragged herself up the wooden stairs with unsteady steps. Once inside her room, she flopped on her bed. She sighed deeply—her mother had not been able to notice any change in her except her off-colour face. She was still shaky and perspiring.

Outside the window of her bedroom, sparrows were chirping noisily. In the distance, a crow cawed relentlessly. She had seen a crow only once or twice but could recognise its call. "A crow cawing relentlessly is a bad omen," her mother had said once but she did not pay much attention to it. "Could she be right? Does it really mean a bad omen?" she thought, "No, no, I'm not superstitious. It is silly to belief such things."

She had heard many tales about crows from her grandmother. Crows got the boon of immortality from Lord Rama for its faithful service while He was in exile. Crows were once very common in Manipur; a menace it surely was. It used to steal and snatch food from the hands of small children. Chicks and ducklings were not safe with a crow around—no chick or duckling that had strayed away from the entourage around its mother could escape the prying eyes of a crow; it would swoop down silently and carry it away.

Crows live in communities and fly around in flocks. Very often, they quarrel among themselves noisily for greater share of food. But, when it comes to a common enemy, all of them flock together to fight. They attack anyone, even man, whoever tries to harm any of them. It surely is a lesson humans have to learn from them.

"Our crows are bigger than the other crows, I had seen outside Manipur, on my pilgrimage to Nabadwip," her grandmother had said once, "Our crow has jet-black iridescent feathers all over its body but the other crow has dull grey feathers on its neck and body. Of course, its head and wings are black . . ."

". . . the caws of our crow have a deeper note than that of the other crow. Crows are able to foresee the future. They had a premonition of the present turmoil in the state and migrated to Bangladesh in the seventies after the civil war there . . ."

An ambiguous explanation, though, Tombi believed everything her grandmother told her about the absence of crows in Manipur till she heard her school teacher—"Pesticides used by farmers in their fields combined with the cutting of trees that serve as the nesting places have wiped out crows." Whatever may be the cause crows have suddenly vanished from Manipur and become almost extinct. Crow is now a very rare bird in Manipur.

Contrary to what her mother had said, the relentless cawing of the crow in the distance was a welcome sound, a melodious uncanny song to unaccustomed ears—it had a soothing effect on Tombi. But, it went farther and farther away till it became only a feeble sound, barely audible. Only the chirping of sparrows could be heard loud and clear, now. Melancholy pervaded her mind when she recollected the excited chirps of a pair of sparrows she had heard during her childhood.

She had spent her childhood at a sparsely populated hamlet comprising of not more than five or six households, a new settlement, not yet granted the status of a village in the census records. Not many children were around, of her age group, there was none. Older children of the other houses had no time to mix and play with her. Most of the time during the day, her parents would be out to work in paddy fields. Her grandmother would sit in a corner of the veranda with a needle and bright coloured silk threads embroidering beautiful designs on the borders of *phige phanek*. Her elder brother was the only person available to play with her. Most of the time, she played with him but he refused to play with her doll, her most prized possession, made from her mother's old clothes by her grandmother.

Once, she saw a young sparrow learning to fly, following its parents. It flew for a short distance and dropped on the ground. She loved the fledgling very much and wanted to own it as her own. She ran after it. Up it flew again chirping loudly only to drop on the ground again a little ahead.

Her parents were away. Her grandmother too was busy with her needlework—she did not have to worry about them. She called her brother. Together, they chased and caught the fledgling. She held the helpless fledgling, shivering with fright and breathing heavily, in her cupped hand and talked to it softly, trying to soothe it. Its alarmed parents flew around her, chirping excitedly. Feeling sorry, her brother told her to let it go but she would not listen. She wanted to keep it as her playmate. In her innocent mind, she imagined and dreamed of many games she would play with it. Near the backdoor, she tied it to a bamboo pole with a string. She sat at a distance and watched it fluttering its tiny wings trying to free itself.

Suddenly a cat appeared out of nowhere and ran off with the fledgling, her dear friend. It gave out a loud shriek before its life ran out. Everything happened so quickly; the cat ran out of sight even before she could get up. Stunned, she jumped and stared agape. Perched on the branch of a plum tree growing in their compound, the poor parents continued to chirp animatedly and Tombi stealthily cried the whole day.

At sunset, she felt a little better and went to their gate made of four bamboo poles placed horizontally at different heights by passing through holes in two wooden posts on either side, to wait for the return of her parents who had gone to market to buy things for *Cheiraoba*, the traditional Manipuri New Year Day. Sitting on the uppermost pole, riding on an imaginary horse, she looked up. The last rays of the setting Sun streaked across the sky. Suddenly she saw a string of pearls up in the sky. She pointed it out to her brother, standing nearby, "Dada, look! A necklace of pearls is drifting across the sky. I wish I had one like that." Her brother laughed aloud and said, "You fool! You and your imagination! It's only a flock of egrets returning home."

The next day her brother cleared a patch near their gate, wiped it clean with mud paste and constructed a mud wall all around it with a small opening on the eastern side. She ran all around collecting wild flowers and decorated the mud wall by sticking the flowers. After that, they together cleared another patch near the bamboo grove at the back of their house and wiped it clean with mud paste but they did not decorate this one with flowers. After completing their job, they ran to other houses and compared their work with what the neighbours had made. Satisfied that theirs was the best, they took bath after fetching water from a pond in their compound and went to kitchen to see what their mother was preparing.

Her mother was arranging the food items, she had laboriously prepared the whole morning, on banana leaves. She put rice, cooked and neatly packed, on a banana leaf cut into round shape and other items in *dona* she had made. With her eyes rolling from side to side, Tombi examined the mouth-watering items, delicacies she did not get to eat everyday—*Mairen-aganba, hangam-champhut, mangal-uti, singju, peruk-kangshu, maroi-bora, iromba-kanchi, chagempomba, kambong-kanghou* and many other items she did not know. She also saw *kusumlei, kombirei* and some other flowers she had never seen before, and varieties of small fruits placed separately on banana leaves. Her mother carefully lifted the arranged items on a big brass plate and handed it over to her father. He went towards the gate, with her and her brother trudging closely behind, prancing around happily.

At the gate, he placed the items, meant to appease evil spirits and ward them off, one by one on the patch they had specially prepared. With folded hands, they prayed to the evil spirits roaming around to accept their offerings and turn away from their family. They repeated the same process at the patch near the bamboo grove at the back of their house.

Only after the traditional offerings were made, the whole family sat together and had a hearty meal.

After lunch, they put on their best dresses to visit her maternal grandparents' house in another village. Only her grandmother stayed behind. They walked along the dusty track leading to the main road to catch a bus. Tombi and her brother jumped from side to side while walking to avoid the ruts on the path made by the wheels of bullock-carts. In the bus, she sat on her father's lap while her mother and brother occupied separate seats.

At her maternal grandparents' house, they presented the gifts they had brought to their grandparents and uncles. Each of them showered them with blessings for a peaceful life and better future. Once the customary service was over, next came the most enjoyable part of *Chieraoba* Tombi had been looking forward to. They went to a nearby hillock. First, they climbed the hillock and prayed at a makeshift temple at the top. After that, they roamed around a fair held in an open field. There, they bought colourful pinwheels and balloons. They returned home after dark, giggling all the way, holding the pinwheels whirling wildly and tugging the balloons tied with threads behind.

Droughts and floods, vagaries of weather played important roles in their lives. When she was nine, a severe drought struck and her parents' income from cultivating rice dwindled to almost nil. They were on the verge of starvation. At the same time, her grandmother became seriously ill and was confined to bed most of the time. Her parents ran hither and thither to borrow money for her grandmother's treatment but they could not save her.

After her grandmother's death, they left their hamlet and came over to Moirang Crossing. There, her parents rented a small house and opened a shop. Tombi and her brother were admitted to a nearby school. To raise capital for the business, they sold off their original homestead. Their business prospered. Within a short span of a few years, they saved enough money to purchase the house they were residing now.

About five years ago, her brother was picked up by security personnel. He never returned home.

One day, late in the night when all of them had gone to bed, they heard gunshots. The shoot-out went on for nearly half an hour. Soon after the sound of the gunshots had died down, heavily armed men in uniform forcibly entered their house and dragged her brother, a student of class X at that time, out of the house without giving any reason. Her parents pleaded and tried to block the way but they were threatened to be shot dead. Pretending to be asleep, she, frightened out of her wits, saw everything from behind the mosquito net draped around the bed.

A brilliant student that he was, his teachers had great expectations of him bringing a good name to the school in the forthcoming High School Leaving Certificate Examination. Her father ran heaven and earth to find out who had arrested him, where he was but he could never trace him. He had become one of the many youths arrested without arrest-memos and not returned.

Thinking about his dear son had taken a heavy toll on Tombi's father's health; he died a heartbroken man. Her mother also had become a nervous wreck but recovered not long after. Now, only Tombi and her mother were left to fend for themselves. Her mother's sole worry was to get her married.

"Tombi . . . if you're feeling better, come and help me."

Her mother's call brought her back to reality. She did not know how long she had been lying on the bed—she had lost the track of time.

When she entered the shop again her mother was busy checking the stock, all the while muttering under her breath, "With them around in the house, I could not go to Imphal to get fresh supplies for the last so many days. At this rate, we have to close the shop and starve to death. By the grace of God they have left today . . . *Hare Krishna . . . Hare Krishna.*"

Busy in what she was doing, her mother did not notice her presence. When she turned around and saw her, she said, "I have to go to Imphal to get fresh supplies for the shop."

"Mama . . ."

"Yes, what's it?"

"They . . ."

"Yes, they have left for good. You need not worry about them for the moment, at least. I have to hurry to Imphal while they are gone. Who knows they may turn up again tonight?"

Tombi shuddered at the mention of their return.

An Imphal bound bus came and stopped on the other side of the road.

"A bus has come, I've to rush. I'll be back before one in the afternoon. You may close the shop and stay upstairs if you wish. But, it's safer to sit in the shop in direct view of everyone. Prepare whatever you like, and eat. Don't wait for me."

While crossing the road, she shouted back, "Be careful."

Tombi silently watched her mother getting on the bus with tightly rolled gunny-bags tucked under her left arm. She pondered how she was toiling to make a living even after all those unfortunate incidents—would it be justified to make her suffer more by disclosing what had happened to her? Would it not hamper her fortitude?

The bus drove off leaving behind a trail of dust and smoke. Tombi slowly sat down on a bench.

She knew many of the regular passengers who used to drop in their shop during the short stopover. One particular young man, working in a government office at Churachandpur, a regular commuter, had caught her fancy. She generally looked forward to staying alone in the shop while her mother was away—she would stealthily scan each and every bus from the corner of her eyes searching for him. On all working days, he also made it a point to drop in their shop to buy something or other on his way to office and back. He was a man of few words but every single word that flowed out from his mouth seemed to speak volumes to her. The sight of him sent her heart racing wild into ecstasy. She had a silent inkling of his reciprocation to her unexpressed desire to be with him alone.

But, that day she was not her usual self. She hated to be left alone. She idly looked around the shop. The almost empty racks seemed to stare back at her mockingly and the incidents of the previous night came back flashing before her murky eyes.

She was now a full-grown woman but her mother kept vigil as if she were a baby. With unruly men around, her mother felt very insecure and was apprehensive about untoward happenings. Safe with her mother, a lioness, guarding her she was lying asleep peacefully. A hand placed on her mouth to stop her from shouting in alarm suddenly woke her.

"Don't panic. It's me . . ."

He was the leader of the three youths who claimed to belong to one of the numerous insurgent groups and had forcibly stayed in their house. They had done so earlier many times. They came and went as they wished. Tombi and her mother were helpless against the heavily armed strangers. They could neither inform their neighbours nor report to the police—it would only create more trouble and complicate the matter. They had had a bitter experience of being harassed by the police when her father reported the arrest of her brother by one of the many groups of security personnel operating in their area. Instead of helping them to trace the whereabouts of her brother, the police charged that her innocent brother must have been a member of an insurgent group to warrant arrest. Her father was detained for a number of days for questioning—he was released only after local *Meira Paibi* intervened.

Tombi still shuddered with fright when she recollected the incidents in the aftermath of the arrest of her brother. All over the state, *Meira Paibis* of different localities had come out in large numbers and staged *dharna* demanding the release of her brother. They had also blocked the roads and organised rallies but to no avail; the whereabouts of her brother could never be known.

Of late, Tombi and her mother stayed aloof from their neighbours only because of the youths—if the news of the presence of the strangers in their house leaked out, Tombi's marriage prospect would be doomed.

Outside it was raining heavily. Tombi's mother, dead tired after the day's hard work, had been trying to keep vigil. But the sound of raindrops falling on the corrugated iron sheet roof served as lullaby and soon put her in a deep slumber.

Pitter-patter went the raindrops and the leader had his way. The noise the raindrops made drowned Tombi's muffled cry—her mother lay asleep peacefully unaware of her struggle. Having had his fill, he soon left leaving behind a devastated Tombi. The lioness had failed to protect her cub. Tombi, her badly mauled cub, lay awake sobbing the whole night.

At dawn, her mother woke up and went down along with the strangers. Tombi waited for her to come up alone but she never did. Early morning customers had kept her busy in the shop.

The sound of trucks speeding towards Churachandpur in convoy suddenly alerted her and sent a chill of apprehension down her spine. On an impulse, she got up to close the shop.

Boom . . . a loud explosion threw her off-balance while she was struggling to close the wooden folding door. The rattle of machine guns followed. It was so close, bullets swished past her. With great difficulty she managed to close the door and ran up to her room. Feeling safe she stretched out on her bed but her heart was still pounding.

Amidst the rattle of machine guns, she heard people shouting and crying in agony. The chaos did not last long—an unearthly silence followed. She prayed for her mother to return safe and sound.

After a while she heard the sound of heavy boots thumping on the ground. Someone knocked heavily on the back door and called out loudly to open but she did not move. Repeated banging at the door was followed by a crashing sound and the clatter of things being thrown around. Their shop below was being ransacked. She was shivering in fright—her teeth clattered. She covered her face with a pillow and tried to control her fear.

Silence followed again but only to be broken soon by the rumbling voice of a man.

"Search all over. We have information—this house is their hideout."

The house shook and rattled as if it too was shuddering in terror when heavy boots stepped on the wooden planks of the stairs.

Everything happened in such a quick succession, Tombi did not get time even to get down from the bed and hide. She froze when three men in uniform entered her room in a flash.

Without a word, whining like animals they jumped on her and pinned her down on the bed. She opened her eyes wide in horror and screamed but no sound came out. One man grasped her hands while another held her legs. She struggled and tried to kick herself free but they were too strong for her. With a cruel smile on his lips, the third mounted her in haste. Unable to bear the pain of the brutal force she fainted almost immediately and lost her consciousness. Unhindered, the men changed positions to release their pent-up fury on her beautiful form sans clothes.

When she came around she was lying alone on her bed, moaning. She felt a burning sensation where the men had touched and defiled her. She heard people shouting and calling her below but she had lost her voice. Numb with ache all over her body, she felt very weak—she was in no condition to get up.

After a while she heard her mother's frantic voice amidst the noise.

"Our bus was detained saying there was a shoot-out here. What happened?"

A number of alarmed people simultaneously trying to relate what had happened caused only noise and confusion.

She broke down in tears and lamented, "O Tombi, my Tombi . . . where are you?"

Hearing her mother's voice gave her courage. She struggled hard to reply. Feigning safe and unharmed, she shouted as loud as she could.

"Mama . . . I'm up here . . . in my room."

13

The Land of Humanoids

Yaima was standing by the side of Bir Tikendrajit Road in Khwairamband Bazar. A blanket of thick mist had engulfed the whole place. His vision was limited to only a few metres ahead of him. Even though the place was crowded, it was unusually quiet. Everyone moved about like mechanical robots programmed to do definite tasks, without making the slightest noise. The thick mist in the height of summer combined with the eerie silence made it a very strange place.

He looked around and examined the place carefully. Yes, it was the same market not very far from his house at Nagamapal. He was sure of it. In the distance he heard the sound of a siren. Everyone ran wild looking for safe hiding places. In no time the place was completely deserted. He was puzzled. He did not know what to do. Someone grabbed his arm from behind and dragged him to a nearby alley. The stranger motioned him to hide behind a wall in the alley. They reached the hiding place in the nick of time. Just then a number of vehicles sped past.

He had a quick glimpse of the vehicles. A white Gypsy, fitted with a siren howling loudly, zoomed past escorting a flagged car. Three other Gypsies followed them. The sound of the siren soon died down in the distance. People came out from hiding and carried on with their activities as if nothing had happened.

Only after everything had become normal, the stranger spoke for the first time with a strange feeble voice.

"It was A-One in the flagged car."

"A-One what?" asked Yaima.

"You don't know A-One! He is the Ruler of this country—a small country surrounded by hills on all sides. My suspicion is confirmed. You are new to this place."

"No, I live at Nagamapal. My house is not very far from here."

"This place may look exactly like the place near your house but it is not the same place."

Yaima could not make out head and tail of what the stranger was saying. He simply kept staring at him. He then noticed that the stranger looked very pale and lifeless just like the dead body he had once seen at the mortuary.

After a brief pause, the stranger spoke again as if he had read Yaima's mind.

"I know what you are thinking—I look like a dead body."

He continued in a hushed tone, "It's not a safe place to talk. Come to my place. I'll explain everything."

The stranger moved ahead a few steps and stood in front of a door that directly opened to the alley. He took out a key from his pocket and unlocked the door. He pushed the door open and went inside. Yaima silently followed him. Once they were inside, the stranger securely bolted the door and motioned Yaima to sit on the only chair in the room. A funny pungent smell filled the room.

Yaima sat on the chair and looked around. It was very dark inside the room. The only source of light was through a long narrow vertical slit in the tightly closed window. The stranger brought a stool made of cane and bamboo. He placed it very close to Yaima and sat on it.

The stranger explained, "This country is ruled by humanoids. They suck human blood—it is their staple diet. They kill human beings for sport. They have made laws and framed rules for the human beings to follow."

He paused for a while to see Yaima's reaction. Yaima remained silent.

"There is no specific law or rule for them. They do whatever they like—there is no one to oppose them. Human beings live at their mercy . . ."

". . . In their social set-up, they are divided into three categories— category A, category B and category C. Each individual is known by a code number."

"What about the human beings here, are they also known by a code number?" Yaima inquired.

The stranger inhaled deeply and gave a sigh of weariness.

"Yes, the humanoids have given a code number to each and every human being in the country. They keep strict vigil over the human beings. No one can escape from this place. We are comparable to the fishes we keep in tanks to be eaten whenever we feel like."

Yaima shuddered in cold sweat.

The stranger went on to explain that in their social hierarchy category A occupied the highest position. The other two categories, B and C had their own clearly defined and well-demarcated areas of operations. A serial number attached to the category to which one belonged, formed the code number of an individual. The serial number signified the power and authority of the individual. A-One occupied the highest position, A-two the next position and so on. Category C had a strict dress code whereas individuals of A and B categories could wear any dress of their choice.

Humanoids belonging to category C roamed the streets to make sure that the human beings respected the laws and rules framed by them. They were responsible for controlling and suppressing any move the human beings might make to overthrow their regime. Category B assisted category A in running the country. They carried out the wishes and directives of category A, who stayed in well-guarded palaces.

Category A humanoids appeared in public on important occasions. On such occasions, at least one member from every family of human beings had to be present lest the whole family would be severely punished.

Yaima found it hard to swallow what the stranger said.

"How can human beings be controlled by humanoids? Human beings are supposed to be the most intelligent and well organised of all the living beings on the surface of the Earth," he argued.

"My dear young man, you are wrong. Human beings may be intelligent but they are not so well organised. They are very selfish. For a few throw away crumbs, some human beings have joined hands with the humanoids. They have sacrificed their own kin for personal benefit and comfort. I know it is hard to believe what I said since you belong to a different place and time."

Suddenly a loud deafening shrill noise filled the air. Yaima jumped up with a start. He blocked his years with his palms.

"That is a signal for the human beings to come and gather at the public ground. A-One is addressing a gathering there to mark the Golden Jubilee of their rule."

Yaima could not hear what the stranger had said. After the noise had died down, he asked, "What was the noise?"

"It is a signal calling the human beings to Polo Ground. All my family members had become prey to the bloodthirsty humanoids. I am the only one left alive. I have to be present at the ground."

The stranger got up and headed for the door.

While opening the door, he said, "You stay back. It is a golden opportunity for you to escape from this wretched place. Everyone will be busy at Polo Ground. No one will notice your absence since you do not have a code number."

After the stranger had left, Yaima opened the door and came out in the open. The fresh air gave him a good relief. He took a deep breath and started walking towards his house. He was now sure that the stranger was a deranged man.

On the road he saw everyone going in the opposite direction, heading for Polo Ground. He turned back and followed them out of curiosity. When he reached Polo Ground, he found that a large number of people had already gathered there. They were eagerly waiting for A-One to address the gathering.

A-One soon arrived escorted by a fleet of cars. When seen at close quarters it turned out that he was someone whom Yaima knew very well. He mused, "When and how did Ta-Boi become A-One, the Chief of humanoids? He was a small-time black marketeer—selling cinema-ticket in black. I used to buy cinema-tickets from him when English movies were regularly screened at Imphal Talkies."

A-One spoke at length about the measures he had taken up for the welfare of the people. The people gave thunderous applause after each and every sentence he said.

Yaima was listening to the speech intently when someone gave a tug from behind. He turned around and saw the same stranger whom he had met earlier.

"Why didn't you follow my advice? There is still time. Everyone will be occupied here for quite a while. You can make good your escape now or never."

He was annoyed with the stranger. He simply was not convinced that Ta-Boi was A-One, the Chief of humanoids. He returned his gaze to A-One and gave a scathing reply.

"How can you say that our Ta-Boi is A-One? Haven't you heard what he said just now? He is working for the welfare of the people."

No response came. He turned around but the stranger was not there—he had vanished in thin air. He turned his face again to watch Ta-Boi but he had also vanished. The crowd was also no longer there. He was standing alone in the middle of Polo Ground.

Out of nowhere, two heavily built personnel in uniform appeared. Both of them were wearing exactly similar dresses. He recollected what the stranger had said, "Category C follows a strict dress code." The two personnel caught hold of him by his arms. He tried to shout but no sound came out. He was frightened out of his wits.

They dragged him to a big palace. After opening the majestic front door of the palace, they entered a very large room. The room was lit by a very bright lone lamp that shone directly above a long and narrow table.

They forcibly laid him on the table. After that, they fastened his wrists and legs with leather belts already fixed on the table for the purpose.

The place reminded him of what he had read about the torture chambers of the middle ages. He could not open his eyes fully with the glaring lamp shining directly above him. After a while he heard someone talking. The voice seemed to be familiar but he could not place it correctly.

Suddenly he recognised the voice, "Oh, yes! It is Ta-Boi's voice."

He glanced sideways to his left and saw Ta-Boi standing beside him. He was rejoiced to see his cool and calm face wearing an angelic smile.

"Alas! I have been saved," he thought.

Ta-Boi put his hands to his face and started peeling the skin. No, he was not peeling his facial skin—he was taking off his mask. It came off easily.

Yaima now could see the real face of Ta-Boi—short forehead, thick brows, small eyes and a small nose with a protruding jaw. He resembled a cross between an ape and a human being.

Ta-Boi bent over him and opened his mouth. Yaima noticed two pointed fangs. He bit him on the neck and started sucking his blood.

Yaima was frozen with fright. He could neither move nor shout. He silently prayed.

"God, benefactor of all, have mercy! Forgive these lowly creatures for their sins and inhuman actions. Change them into human beings so that they can undo their past misdeeds and serve the people for a better tomorrow."

"Oh my God, save the country from these blood suckers!"

He was in cold sweat. He slowly opened his eyes. He was lying on the bed. The bedside lamp was directly focused on his face. He had fallen asleep while reading the day's newspaper. He slowly turned to his side and saw the newspaper lying on the floor beside the bed.

He then saw the sketch of an ape-like creature on the newspaper, an artist's impression—short forehead, thick brows, small eyes and a small nose with a protruding jaw. Under a caption in bold letters, "**Missing link unearthed**," it was written, "*Fossilised skull of an ape-like creature found. Palaeontologists claim that the skull belonged to a humanoid that once roamed the Earth in pre-historic times . . .*"

Yaima was now wide-awake.

"Thank God! It was only a dream."

14

The Flight

During the last three months I have been away from home, I have severed myself completely from my roots in Manipur, my native place. My tight schedule and heavy engagements plus the difference in time have often prevented me from calling my family on phone. It may also be put this way, there is no one left in the family to speak to. My parents have expired long ago. I have no brother, have a sister only, my big sister who is married and settled in Mumbai. I have not bothered about calling and disturbing her at odd hours. She already knows what I am doing and where I am going. With a family to look after, she is busy in her own way. Still single at forty-five, I feel, I am out to conquer the world with the vigour of a teenager, no strings attached, no bindings and no mid-life blues people of my age talk about so often. But, I still cannot keep my thoughts away from home forever. At times, a strange feeling overcomes me, I have left behind a part of me, and I sense something or some part of life is missing.

If I may be allowed to count all the things that are dear to me then my family consists of my dog and my bonsai specimens. I may also add Nishikanta, a man originally from Bangladesh, who lives in our house. Well, he certainly does the odd jobs around the house but he is not a domestic help, I would rather call him my big brother. He is the only person with whom I had spoken on phone. Only on three occasions I had called him, one from Delhi, another from Singapore and the last one from London, to inform my whereabouts and inquire about his well-being.

Medium in stature, lean and thin, he hails from Bishgaon, a village located in the Sylhet alluvial plains in the northeastern part of Bangladesh. He looks much older than his age of fifty-five something but his dynamism defies his appearance. Still amazingly strong, he is very agile and swift in his movements. The present-day chocolate sucking flabby youths, who hanker for fast food only, can nowhere match him in physical work. A man of principle, he never says anything unless spoken to.

He had lost all the members of his family, his newly married wife, his parents, two brothers and a younger sister in the ensuing eight months of martial rule and sporadic firing by West Pakistan's army under the chief martial law administrator and president, General Agha Mohammad Yahya Khan before Bangladesh gained independence from Pakistan in December 1971. Memory of the night when his young wife and sister were dragged away by Pakistani soldiers before their house was torched is still fresh in his mind. After two days, their mutilated bodies were found near a drain. All the other members of his family fell prey to the machinegun bullets that rained from all directions when they ran out of the house to escape from the inferno. Their wails still continue to ring in his ears and haunt him. He had saved himself by hiding in a ditch.

He fled the country along with the few survivors of his village and entered Tripura, a tiny state on the Indian side, after crossing the border. He stayed in Agartala, the capital of Tripura, for a number of years doing odd jobs to survive. Even after the war was over he never returned home. Quite young I was, when he came to our house I could not comprehend fully the anguish he must have felt at the loss of his family. Stranded now as I am, alone in a foreign country far away from home, I cannot help but wonder how lonely he must be without his dear ones all these years. Life has been very cruel to him. It may be the reason why he always wears a serious face.

He was brought to Imphal by a goldsmith who used to frequent to Tripura. He worked under him as an apprentice but did not make much progress. My mother met him in the goldsmith's shop when she went there to order some gold ornaments for my sister. Coming to know about his lack of interest in working as a goldsmith and also on learning that he is a Manipuri like us but from Bangladesh prompted mother to offer him to come and stay with us. May be she was overwhelmed with fellow feeling. He readily accepted the offer. Since then he has been living in our house.

I have taught him the finer techniques of gardening and training of plants to enable him to take care of my bonsai specimens in my absence. He is now skilled in the art, can rightly be called a bonsai artist. He also runs the house so well—with him around I have nothing to worry about. Before living home I gave him three signed and post-dated cheques to enable him to withdraw money from my account in the bank whenever the need arises.

Now that I am waiting to board my flight to Delhi, British Airways Flight BA 143, excitement runs high. I have sauntered all over the departure terminal, peeking into the glass windows of stores and admiring the curios on display. I have already done the last minute purchase—bought only a paperback. I don't need nor can afford to buy any of the classy stuffs sold in the stores. My luggage searched, my ticket torn and my name already punched into the computer, the routine checks are over. At the departure terminal, the process is much faster— the hassle of walking along a long maze of zigzag passage following directions to the immigration counter at the arrival terminal is not there. Of course, the inconvenience and physical strain of walking and pushing the luggage trolley when I arrived was greatly reduced by the travelators laid along the sidewalk.

I find airports, designed to a very high standard of space and decor, less melodramatic in the sense railway and bus stations are, where near and dear ones linger around till the last moment of departure. I hate to bid last minute farewell to anyone. Departure from airport is more convenient and thrilling for me who refuses to be dragged into hanky-panky with anyone.

Boarding light seems to be taking forever to come on. The moment I entered Terminal 4 of Heathrow Airport, I started counting the minutes. From Leyton I had caught the tube at Walthamstow Central, the easternmost terminal along the Victoria line and changed to Picadilly line at Green Park to come to Heathrow. I covered the distance from the Motel to the tube station in a minicab.

Minutes tick by and 'forever' comes to an end, the boarding light starts blinking and I board the aircraft. Inside the bird I take my seat, a window seat. A portly brown man of undeterminable age, his forehead marked with a white paste in the centre, joins me in the aisle seat. He nods his head and joins his palms to greet me. A friendly gesture? Yes, I believe so. I too nod my head and press my palms together to return the greeting but do not speak a word. No one turns up to occupy the seat between us. Both the rows of seats in front and behind are also empty. At this time of the year, the beginning of September, not many passengers are on board the flight—off-season for tourists coming to visit India.

I press my face against the glass window to watch the outside scene. On the tarmac, rows of jetliners are parked; undoubtedly the maximum number of aircrafts I have seen parked at one place.

Airborne, I watch the fascinating sight. Down below, London is miniaturising. Everything is scaled down in perfect proportion as in a large exhibition model of the layout of a town. Some of the buildings and monuments stand out perfectly because of their exemplary designs and shapes, reminding me of my bonsai specimens. The bird climbs up higher and higher, and penetrates the white fluffy clouds. Once it reaches above the clouds, nothing except the clouds can be seen and I pull down the shade to shield my eyes from the glaring light reflected by the clouds.

Stewardesses start trundling the passage with drink trolleys. I excuse myself for I fear drinks may spoil my reverie I plan to slip into. I plug in the stereo and punch the buttons to select a number. I am not a music fan nor do I have the taste for any particular form of music. Still, I find soft music very soothing. Who doesn't? I close my eyes and let myself to be drowned in subtle instrumental music, allowing it to permeate every limb of my body. In serene contemplation, I put my thought in reverse gears and travel backward in time.

I have a permanent home and address at Imphal and I do get mails all right but seldom in time. Many more mails might have been lost on the way. I have no idea of the undelivered mails for I never got them. In this God forsaken north-eastern corner of India, postal service goes at a snail's pace. It had really hampered the progress of my work. Many a time, my time-bound mails were delivered after the stipulated time. Getting mails in time had really been a problem till I acquired my permanent one line address, my e-mail address, an address without address. With my e-mail address, I never miss my mails, now.

Of late, wandering through cyberspace has become my favourite pastime. Whenever I am free, I go globetrotting and fly around the world with the index finger placed on the mouse button. With a click I can reach anywhere. There is so much to see and learn—use a search engine, type any word or topic in the search window and click the mouse button to launch the search, rest is magic, within seconds a bewildering number of links to websites containing the word or topic will pop up on the screen. I prefer 'google' to search.

Using cyberspace has saved me considerable time. I no longer take voluminous books out of shelves and open the pages. Of course, I still refer books for in-depth study. In Imphal, my chaotic hometown, everyone seems to be an expert in his or her own way, not many are willing to listen to my positive or constructive suggestions for the betterment of the society. I have done some groundwork by carrying out surveys on my own and postulated a number of theories and suggestions but there is no taker. I have presented a number of papers in seminars but with no positive result. Then why don't I give up, a question I often ask myself, of which I have found neither the answer nor the courage, yet. It gives me immense pain and pricks my brain to see so many people suffering all around me. I must do something for them. Cyberspace has helped me and come to my rescue.

The latest survey I had conducted on my own was on Social Exclusion vis-a-vis Disparity in Income. I prepared a questionnaire, interviewed a large number of people from all walks of life and jotted down their answers and suggestions. I tabulated my findings, prepared graphs and wrote a paper. I e-mailed it to a number of publishers that specialise in Social Science. Ultimately, it was published in a journal brought out by a private foundation and I got instant recognition. I was invited to attend one week's training course conducted by the foundation at Kolkata. We attended lectures by experts. The participants were broken up into groups of fours and made to visit different localities to interview a number people and prepare a paper on the findings. It was quite an experience. After that I attended a workshop of the same duration conducted by the same foundation at Chennai.

Not long after came my break to conduct surveys at three different places, New Delhi, Singapore and London, spread over three different countries, over a period of three months. For it, I had to work with three other persons all form different countries, Damrong from Thailand, Srinivasan from Singapore and Jameson from South Africa. This time, we were allowed to work independently on our own updating a General Household Survey on 'Immigration and Homogeneity in Multiracial Population' conducted much earlier. Every week we had to submit the progress of our work.

In New Delhi our survey mainly concentrated in the areas where refugees from Bangladesh and Tibet have settled whereas in Singapore, the "Lion City," we covered the minorities of Malays and Indians, mostly.

Only after reaching London, I realised how and why the foundation had chosen us, from outside Europe, to do the follow-up surveys. In London, the culmination point of migration from many African and Asian countries, the immigrants are reluctant to answer many of the questions put to them by Europeans. But, they opened their hearts out to us.

After submitting the final report, we were free to do as we please and we parted ways. I decided to stay back in London for two more days to visit all the interesting places. Well, I had already sorted out the problem of finding a place to stay within my means. For the survey we conducted, we had to visit many areas with mixed population. For quite a number of days we concentrated in Leyton, a quiet and peaceful area not so crowded but with a sizeable mixed population. There, I saw a motel, Sleeping Beauty Motel, a lovely place where I can afford to stay. On the first day, sitting atop an open-topped double-decker bus, I covered many important places on a conducted tour. I saw Buckingham Palace, Piccadilly Circus, Trafalgar Square, Big Ben and the Houses of Parliament, London bridge and Westminster Abbey to name a few. On the second day I purchased a one-day LT card and explored London on my own with the help of a guidebook. At Madame Tussauds and London Planetarium, I met many important personalities of the world. There, I attended the Garden Party where I stood side-by-side many legends of the time and spent macabre hours in the Chamber of Horrors. Now, I can swear I have seen London if not from close quarters.

My only link with my native place during the surveys was the news-websites. Daily, I used to browse and open websites for any news about my hometown after the day's works were over. I went through every single line of the postings in the websites, everyday. My favourite websites are 'e-pao.net' and 'kanglaonline.com', two websites that carry news relating to my place. Surprisingly, during the last two months, news of my insignificant hometown infested with insurgents and forgotten by most people around the globe had made the headlines in many news-websites. During my absence several unthinkable incidents had happened. On July 15, 2004, twelve women made history by protesting in front of the Kangla gate, a place sacred to many, with their long tresses let loose and not a stitch on. They had shouted slogans to do justice and punish the killers of Thangjam Manorama who met a gruesome end to her life while in the custody of the Assam Rifles, and to remove Armed Forces Special Powers Act, an act misused by security personnel time after time to torture and kill innocents on the plea of fishing out insurgents. Pebam Chitaranjan, a student leader, had immolated himself as a protest against the killings of Thangjam Manorama and Jamkholet Khongsai, a Pastor, and human rights violation by security personnel. The whole of my native place, otherwise peaceful, is now in turmoil. What has come over it? It is hard to fathom.

It appears that people around the globe have started noticing our plight and the extreme conditions under which we have been living so far. Any action under the existing theoretical laws may not be able to solve the numerous problems we are facing. We have to resort to a pragmatic approach and make suitable amendments in the existing laws. But, who will take the initiatives?

"Welcome, on board Mr. Sanatomba!"

Startled, I open my eyes. Did I hear someone calling my name? Yes, I am sure someone called me. I look around. My neighbour is resting peacefully in his seat with his eyes closed, possibly sleeping. The stewardesses are nowhere to be seen. May be, I am too tired, fatigue is eating into my brain and I am hearing things. I close my eyes again, ready to go back to my reverie.

"Surprised, aren't you? I have many things to tell you."

This time, I heard the voice loud and clear above the music. It was coming through the headphones.

"We have chosen you after carefully checking your antecedents to be the witness of a scientific experiment. Coming from Manipur, a nondescript place in a secluded corner of the earth, a will to work for the betterment of the mankind, a sincere and hardworking man, who could be a better witness?"

Puzzled, I push the buttons to switch over to another channel but the voice is still there.

"We and you together will make history. Sounds interesting, isn't it?"

It makes a brief pause as if waiting for my answer, but I remain silent.

"Well, I'll come to the experiment slowly. First, let me introduce myself. I head a small group of dedicated men, a private group. My men refer to me as Chairman. I am also known by many names. You are free to address me by whatever name you like, I'll remain the same."

A hissing noise like the one heard on a radio set when a station is not properly tuned in is heard and then everything becomes silent. After a while, only the music starts coming through the headphones like before. The voice has already interrupted my reverie. Was it some kind of a practical joke someone on board the flight was playing or have I gone out of my head? I see no reason for either to be true. I do not know anyone on board the flight and I am wide-awake, perfectly sane, not sleeping and dreaming.

All of a sudden the voice starts booming through the headphones again. This time there is a slight tinge of excitement in the speech.

"The first experiment starts within twenty seconds from now. Unfold the screen on the back of the seat before you and watch."

I do as I am told. I unfold the screen but nothing except the aircraft following the dotted flight path can be seen.

"Now the aircraft is flying at an altitude of 10 kilometres and cruising at a speed of 900 kilometers per hour. Do you have any idea how much it will be away from its path if it deviates from the path by 15 degrees and continue to fly for 2 minutes? 7.76 kilometers, to be exact. It is precisely what is going to happen within a couple of seconds."

I keep watching the screen intently and the voice starts counting backwards.

"Ten, nine, eight . . . two, one, now."

I notice a slight jerk in the image of the aircraft on the screen. Then it moves slightly away from the flight path. I count the minutes. At the end of two minutes, the deviation made by the aircraft from the flight path on the screen is so small I would not have noticed it had I not watched it so keenly.

"Congratulate us! The experiment was a success. Now the aircraft will be brought back to its normal course."

The voice becomes silent once more and music starts pouring out from the headphones but what it had said keeps echoing inside my head. Pushing a trolley, two stewardesses start serving food. I unfold my table and accept the food packet handed over by one of the stewardesses. The sight of them gives me some relief. Sighing deeply, I stretch my hands and legs to ease the numbness in my body.

While conducting the surveys, even during the two days when I had stayed behind to see London, time had been so precious I could not waste even a single minute. I grabbed and ate whatever was readily available and continued with what I was doing. In a way I had completely neglected and forgotten about food. Vegetarian cuisine—roti, cooked vegetables, fruit salad and sweetmeats, the Indian dishes served for me seem to be a royal treat after surviving on ready-to-eat packed foods for the last three months. But, after the first bite, the echo of the voice nagging in my brain makes the food tasteless. I push away the food tray and unplug the headphones and take it off.

A severe headache suddenly starts splitting my head. A stewardess comes along and I ask for plain water. She hands me over a small bottle of water. I suppose water is the best remedy, I simply cannot think of taking fruit juice or any other drink with the headache on. I open the bottle and take a sip. I feel slightly better and gulp down two more mouthfuls. I sense the water passing through my gullet and then entering my stomach, pleasantly cooling every part of the body it passes around. The coolness spreads upwards to my head. My headache vanishes as suddenly as it had appeared. The water has done the trick. Of course, 'Water is the elixir of life.'

Feeling better, I try to pick up my reverie from where I had left. What was I thinking about? The survey? No. London? No. Oh yes, now I remember, I was pondering about the troubles in my native place. Such a small place with so many problems! The problems keep multiplying. It is really frustrating to see Manipur being torn to pieces but I can't help. I'm a nonentity—no one will listen to me.

I tell myself, it's better to get some sleep than keep worrying. I straighten out the seat a bit and rest my head on a pillow and try to close my eyes. But, the news of the troubles in Manipur keep coming back. I fold the seat upright again. Unable to do anything, I consider plugging in music again but thinking about the voice stops me short. Was the voice really there or was it my imagination?

This time the voice may not be there. I reluctantly put the headphones on and plug it in. Once more I push the buttons at random to select a beautiful piece of music and adjust the volume to a comfortable level. Having made my choice, I slowly close my eyes and let the music drift me along. Nothing happens for a long time—only a melodious composition wafting around. And the voice—I must have been hallucinating. In no time the music lulls me into a deep slumber.

I open my eyes at the announcement for landing. The news about reaching Delhi and the restful sleep have refreshed me. The plane is now hovering over Delhi with the soft humming of melodious music in my ears. I realise, I must have been wearing the headphones even in my sleep.

"Mr. Sanatomba, now the second and the final experiment is about to begin. Listen carefully and watch it happen." The voice, coming again, gives me a jolt.

"The landing gears will fail to open and the plane will hover longer than it should."

In spite of the air-conditioned interior, I am perspiring—what if the landing gears fail to open? The only alternative is to crash land. My undergarments are already soaked in sweat and I feel like letting out a loud yell to ease the tension. But, I hold back lest people will think I have gone mad. I turn to look at my neighbour. He is sitting calmly, a faint smile playing on his lips and no sign of anxiety on his face. Lost in pleasant thoughts? Perhaps.

"You need not be alarmed. The landing gears will open at the third attempt and the plane will land safely."

I heave a sigh of relief.

Like the voice has said, the plane hovers for a long time before it makes a perfect landing. It starts taxing to the international terminal and I sit calmly thinking, the trauma is over, now. But I keep wearing the headphones for I want the voice to come back and explain me everything, if at all it has not been my imagination.

"The second experiment was also a success," booms the voice again. But, this time there is no excitement in its tone.

"We are experimenting with controlling the bird, without our presence in the cockpit or in the aircraft to be more precise. Thanks to computerisation and automation of aircrafts that have made it possible. Now, we can control any aircraft from anywhere in the world . . ."

". . . Interested to know how we controlled the bird? It's simple . . ."

". . . Well, we can intercept and hook on to any transmission channel, signal or mode of communication, and superimpose our command . . ."

". . . The flight data recorder has recorded all the data. The cockpit voice recorder has recorded my voice. Now, we have the documentary proof of controlling the aircraft without our physical presence inside it. And you, Mr. Sanatomba, are our precious witness, the only witness. Thank you for being so patient and bearing with us. Farewell, Mr. Sanatomba!"

The aircraft comes to a halt. My neighbour gets up, turns to me with his palms joined together and nods his head—a farewell greeting. I too reciprocate in the same manner mechanically but I cannot kick off the thought lingering in my head.

"What if the know-how lands in the hands of terrorists?"

15

Companion

Loneliness is one thing, being alone another. One can feel lonely anywhere even in the midst of crowd. Many people like to stay in the crowd, surrounded by people but at times I enjoy and wish to be left alone, on my own without others disturbing me and distracting my mind. I have an urge to write. To escape from the melancholies of life I indulge in creative writing, fiction or whatever you may call it. However it does not necessarily mean that life is full of melancholies; it has brighter sides too. Through my writings I can do and achieve many things, which I otherwise would not be able to accomplish and pull off in real life. So to say I can strike the point home through it. Writing gives me immense satisfaction, solace, tranquillity and peace of mind in this chaotic world where venality, hypocrisy, brutality and what not, other than love, companionship, compatibility and coexistence have become the very essence of life and survival.

Opinion differs from person to person and I respect others' opinions. When we see a red flower, everyone will agree it is a flower and its colour is red. The consensus may end there. Someone will say it is beautiful while another may say it is not. When I write I do write for myself only, I suppose it is the best way to write for I do not know others' likes and dislikes. Furthermore, it is beyond my capability to please one and all. If others appreciate my writing, I am fortunate otherwise also it gives me a thrill to spell out what my inner voice commands me to do.

While writing I need to contemplate and concentrate so that the characters appear before my eyes in the correct situations enacting the scenes and I can describe it comprehensively. A night owl, I certainly am, only when I am alone in the dead of night my characters come alive.

I was sitting in front of my computer furiously punching the keys, trying to write a story . . .

. . . A pair of pigeons, blue rock pigeons, had made the balcony of the third floor flat their home. Intruders? Certainly not, rather we were the intruders for the pigeons had been living in the area long before we came. Only three months back, I had moved in the flat, located in a residential block, not very far from my office.

After my transfer to Bangalore, I was staying in a hostel provided by the company where I worked. But, staying in a hostel after one started working was disagreeable to me—it hurt my self-esteem. Nevertheless, I was a bit reluctant to stay alone in a flat.

Victor, a colleague of mine, a newcomer to the city and a bachelor like me, suggested for sharing a rented flat, as if he had read my mind. I jumped at the proposal but the problem of finding a flat still loomed large. Coming to know of our problem, a senior colleague advised, "A new residential complex is coming up ten minutes walk from here. Some of the blocks are ready. If you go there and inquire, you may find someone willing to let out a flat on rent."

That very day, following the advice, we proceeded on foot to the new residential complex after office. There we met an old lady who owned two adjacent flats. A nice lady with shrunken eyes, dog-weary in trying to persuade her two sons who stayed in Mumbai to come and stay with her, sparkled the moment she saw us. We reminded her of her sons. She was more than willing to let out one of the flats to us, in a way our presence there would make her feel secure as if her sons were near her.

In the flat, we occupied two separate rooms sharing a common balcony. To bring some life and greenery to the balcony, I bought five potted plants, taking meticulous care to choose only those plants that can survive long without watering and grow well with little attention— weeping fig, nolina palm, dumb cane, aluminium plant and wandering jew. I stood the pots in trays that can hold water for a considerable period of time. Pouring water into the trays once in a while, not watering the soil directly from top was all the care I had to take. The balcony seemed to have come alive all of a sudden with the foliage gently swaying in the breeze.

Early in the morning, the very next day after putting the potted plants on the balcony, I was woken up by a deep-throated call 'gootr-goo, gootr-goo'. Through the glass window that opened out to the balcony, I saw a pair of pigeons drenched in the mellow morning light. One of the pigeons was sleeking its plumage, stretching the head forward showing glistening metallic green, purple and magenta sheen feathers on the neck, and partially raising the wings. The other was sitting indifferently, caring little to what its mate was doing. With a mild feeling of exhilaration, I sat up on my bed and watched the love-game the pair was playing. After a few minutes much to my disappointment the pair flew off.

That day after office, intently wishing the pair to return again the next morning I purchased chickpeas and maize to feed the pigeons. Before retiring to bed I put the chickpeas and maize in separate bowls and placed it in the balcony. The pair returned again the following morning. After that, each morning I keenly watched the developments. The pair brought a few twigs and made a nest in the pot with the weeping fig.

The pigeons reminded me of the bygone days of my childhood in Imphal. In our house at Lamphelpat, we kept a pair of white pigeons. It was given to my mother, a physician, by an old man saying that keeping a pair of white pigeons in the house would bring good luck and ward off evil spirits. The pair became my friend, my playmate and my companion.

How and when did I turn into a man from a boy? The question still perturbs me. I suppose a boy turns into a man when the need arises, not as the boy grows. In my case the need arose quite early in my life. Even in my school uniform I felt as if I were a man in the garb of a boy. When I became aware, there were only three of us in the family, mother, my big sister and I. As far as I remember I have always been a man, a precious one. My father was away in another city. I have seen him only two or three times. I don't know when my parents were separated. Being the only male member in the family I was always treated as a man not as a child. I sense I have skipped my childhood.

What is the essence of life? I have no idea. The only thing that bothers me most is that there are so many things I have to accomplish. Every day seems to be a new beginning, today, the present, is the only time that belongs to me; yesterday, a time lost and tomorrow, a nagging future. I have to strive for the best today. The wheel of time rolls on. Who knows what the future holds for me?

The white pigeons of my childhood seemed to have reincarnated as blue rock pigeons . . .

I yawned as drowsiness tried to distract me but I was determined to complete the story.

"So you're writing a story."

It gave me a mild shock to feel the presence of someone in the room and hear him so close for I had already locked both the front and back doors downstairs from inside. After making sure everyone in the family had gone to sleep and no one was there to disturb me, I had come to my study on the first floor and sitting in front of my computer started punching the keys.

It was a very familiar voice but still I had trouble in recognising its owner. I turned around to see who he was. He was standing in the shade. I could not see his face clearly—my eyes having been glued to the computer screen for a long time I had trouble in adjusting to the poor light in the corner.

"How did you come inside?"

Pat came the reply, "How surprising! How I came inside? This is my room."

I got more perplexed. He came closer and softly patted me on my back but I still could not see his face properly.

"To cut the story short, it is I who have been writing the stories for you," he continued, "You simply type out the words and call the story yours."

I blurted out, "How is it possible?"

He coolly said, "Calm down, don't get excited. At this rate you won't be able to make any headway. For the time being simply presume that we share the room. It belongs to both of us."

I still could not make head or tail of what he was saying. The voice was so familiar that I could not straightway deny his claims. His interruption had caused me to forget what I was writing.

"Now, coming to the point, why do you write at all?"

I retorted, "Why do I write, a funny question indeed! Just now you told me you do the writing for me. Well, if you don't know, writing gives me immense satisfaction. It is the only thing I can do without the help of others or disturbing them."

He remained silent for quite a while. Then, he continued, "You have been writing about pigeons. Why not write about the so many things happening around you?"

I said, "I write whatever strikes me or comes to my mind. I have no particular choice as to the subject of my writing."

He laughed aloud and said, "You mean you want to escape from the melancholies of life. Isn't it?"

Not knowing what to say I simply nodded my head.

"You are perfectly right. Nobody wants to indulge in something he or she detests—everyone starts looking for ways and means of escaping from it. In your case writing is an escape. But still if all of us discard the reality, then reality itself will cease to exist. Mirage will come in to play and replace reality."

I could no longer remain silent. To strike my point home, I said, "I write fictions. You can say fictions are reflections of reality. If I write about only the things that are happening around us then my creative writings will turn out to be nothing but simple reports of facts. There will be no difference or distinction between newspaper reports and creative writings."

He chuckled and said, "Who says newspaper reports are not fictions? Are all the reports published in the newspapers true? Certainly not. See, if you note down every detail of our conversation then what will you call it—a report or a creative piece?"

Yawning noisily, without waiting for my answer, he slowly walked over to the divan placed against the wall and lay down face up. Relieved that he was no longer disturbing me, I kept punching the keys till the small hours.

When I slowly opened my eyes, I was lying in supine position on the divan. My eyes still cloudy and my head unclear, I went to bathroom and splashed water on my face. Drowsiness instantly left me and I became alert. I held my face up and looked into the mirror. There, he was standing before me with a discomfited smile on his lips, a very perturbing one. Presently, I recollected the one who had disturbed me while I was sitting in front of my computer. I could recognise him immediately even if I had not seen his face clearly at that time.

I said, "What are you doing here? Trying to upset me again?"

"Didn't I tell you, this is my house? I live here."

I could not help but wonder aloud, "But that does not mean that you have to follow me wherever I go."

"I'm equally helpless. I have been made to follow you everywhere— you're my destiny."

I turned my face away, went to the study and sat before my computer. Surprisingly it was 'on and sleeping'. I must have forgotten to switch it off. The moment I touched the keys it came alive. Another surprise was in store for me—my conversation with the stranger was already typed into the computer. Each and every word we had said was neatly recorded in writing.

I scrolled up and down the pages. The story I had written was also there, very much, only to be followed by our conversation. I thought of deleting the portion containing the records of our conversation—it would spoil the story, no head or tail, an abrupt insertion. But something at the back of my mind kept telling me, "Don't delete. Keep it."

And, I resumed punching the keys once more to complete the story I had started writing . . .

16

The Rickety Bamboo Fort

A faint streak of light started showing above the hills, painting the eastern sky with a hue of flame red colour. Darkness of the night had shied away as a new day dawned. The usually quiet and peaceful hamlet in a far corner of the valley had been transformed into a noisy and chaotic place by a trivial incident of the previous night. Everyone was panicky and worried about the incident that had suddenly disturbed their peaceful lives. They abandoned their work and gathered at the grazing-ground, which also served as the meeting place, to settle an important issue that had been bothering them for a long time. All of them were waiting patiently for the arrival of Tomchou, the wise grand old man, to hear his advice and suggestions. The fate of the hamlet lay on him.

While waiting for his arrival, the panic stricken rustic folks were talking about the imminent doomsday, which they thought would come sooner than they had expected.

"We are living at the vague end of *Kali Yug*. A new *Yug* will soon start. It is already foretold that the present world will be completely devastated to pave way for the new *Yug*."

"*Yama-Doots* have already arrived from the Netherworld to call back all the living beings. They will drag everyone back to the Land of Dead. However pious one may be, there is no escape from their clutches."

"Yes, this time no one can escape. I have survived the Great Second World War. When aeroplanes first started bombing, I thought that the end of the World had come. We survived the bombing raids by taking shelter in trenches but there is no means or way to escape from the *Yama-Doots.*"

"In those days, we could very easily make out who was who and keep our distance from the fighting men."

"Now, everything has changed. We don't know who is who. Who is fighting whom? We are caught unaware amidst the crossfire. Both the sides accuse us of taking the other's side."

"Our lives are in their hands. They can do whatever they like. There is no one to stop them. You have no idea of what I had experienced. I have never been humiliated before in my life like they had done. At one point I was even confused whether I was still a human being or an animal. How I had wished to die to be free from the mental as well as physical tortures!"

In the distance, they saw an old man walking on three, coming towards them. They stopped talking and turned their attention to the road. They recognised him. He was the one all of them had so eagerly been waiting for. Tomchou, bent with age, came slowly on foot with the help of his walking stick.

He was the one who had first settled at the place near the foot of the hills after leaving the crowded township further up along the main road—the founder of the hamlet. Others had followed suit. It was said that he could predict the Future accurately. The simple superstitious rustic folks obeyed whatever he asked them to do. No one, except a handful few youths, who were fortunate enough to have been exposed to the light of modern education, had the courage to question his words and challenge his authority. The educated youths cast their influence on the other youths of the settlement.

The younger generation was eager to adopt the western life-style and discard their old ways, which they called 'primitive'. They refused to listen to the advice of the elders, conflict of thoughts—generation gap. They were not interested to toil in the paddy fields and orchards, which provided them enough income to sustain themselves. They were tempted by easy-money and carefree lives. All of them, except a handful few, had left the settlement looking for greener pastures. The hamlet was on the verge of extinction.

On his arrival, Tomchou took the centre-stage. Everyone was all ears to hear what he had to say. He spoke as loudly as he could in his feeble voice.

"My dear countrymen thank you very much for giving me this opportunity to express my views on the prevailing situation. We are passing through a very bad phase of time. I am very old. I have lived all these years with the hope of seeing our lovely hamlet prosper. Alas, when my end is in sight all my dreams have been shattered!"

He paused for breath.

"Before we put the blame on others, we have to think what our own children have done for us. All of them have discarded and left us to fend for ourselves in our old age, knowing very well that there is no one to look after us."

He wiped his tears and continued.

"The future of our hamlet is bleak. I, personally, thought that our children would work hard for the betterment of the hamlet but they have thrown us into the jaws of a slow but painful death—that's all they have done for us. They have squeezed and extracted whatever little we had. We have also willingly offered them everything in our capacity with the hope of seeing a better future of our hamlet. What have they given us in return except fighting among themselves for a greater share of the booty? They have squandered all our hard-earned money. Our children have become our worst enemies. I am ashamed of them."

He paused again to see the reaction of what he had said. No one uttered even a single word. All of them hung their heads in shame. When he continued again there was a renewed vigour in his voice.

"We shouldn't lose our hope yet. There is still time to undo the mistakes of our children. We have to work hard and face boldly whatever may come our way. We still have our land, the paddy fields and orchards. All our lives we have toiled to feed the thankless lots. We need not worry for those who think the least for us. They have deceived us. They have forgotten there is God, who sees everything. I am sure God will never forgive them for what they have done to us. Let them reap the fruits of their labour."

"They and their virtues bother me the least. They would never listen to our warnings. *Yama-doots* are after them. Many of them have already paid dearly for their sins. The days of the remaining few are also numbered."

"They think they can buy the world with the easy-money they have hoarded. How foolish they are! All they have bought with their easy-money is trouble. I am sorry that some of us had to undergo physical as well as mental agony only because of showing our hospitality to them."

The long speech seemed to be quite taxing on old and weak Tomchou. He took a break to recuperate his strength.

Someone from the crowd said, "We thought that they would never set their feet here again after the last incident but they have come back again. Last night all of us heard their truck passing through our hamlet, heading for the hills. They will return soon. *Yama-Doots* may come again chasing after them. God knows what they will do this time!"

So, it was the sound of a truck plying on the road running through the middle of the hamlet the previous night that had kept the whole hamlet awake. The villagers had every reason to be frightened at the sound of the truck. The road was used by a gang of armed men as a secret route to smuggle in contraband goods from across the country and distribute it to other parts of the country. Many young men who had left the hamlet to seek their fortunes elsewhere were members of the gang. They were the ones who had extracted money from the poor villagers to raise the capital for their illicit trade. They earned a lot, lived in style and spent lavishly while the poor villagers had to toil day and night to keep themselves alive.

Once, a truck carrying full load of *ganja* broke down in the middle of the hamlet. The innocent and unsuspecting villagers helped to unload the *ganja* and store it in one of the houses in the hamlet while the truck was sent to town for repairs. The law enforcers got a hint and raided the hamlet. The villager in whose house the *ganja* was stored was arrested and questioned. He languished in jail for a long time on the charge of helping the gang. No sooner his ordeal with the law enforcers was over then the poor villager had to face and suffer at the hands of the gang. They charged him that he had informed the authorities and beat him blue. Had not the woman-folks of the hamlet intervened they would have finished him off. After that incident the gang had not surfaced again in the hamlet for a long time.

A single question put by the worried villagers in unison echoed in air, "What are we supposed to do now?"

Tomchou replied, "We have to make a sacrifice. The road, which we had built laboriously to ease the transportation problems, has to go. We will divert the irrigation canal by cutting through the road. Over the canal we will build a bamboo bridge."

"Yea, yea," everyone shouted in agreement.

They set to task immediately. By evening, they finished their job. They had cut a wide canal through the road. Over the canal they had built a rickety bamboo bridge—their bamboo fort.

17

Asleep in a box

The much-awaited dark monsoon clouds came, lashing with long whips of rain, trying to punish only the poor and homeless. It had hidden and humbled even the mighty Sun. The incessant rain had soaked everything around but could not dampen Sakhi's spirit. She was busy in the kitchen trying to light a fire in the hearth and cook the last handful of rice left in the house to feed her hungry children at least a morsel of food before putting them to sleep. She pushed the rain soaked firewood into the hearth and went on blowing hard with all her might after inhaling deeply to fully inflate her lungs. The simple task of making a fire in the hearth had now become a Herculean task for her. The baby on her back, her youngest son, had not stopped crying, yet. She was at her wit's end. She could neither console her hungry son nor light a fire.

She got up and brought a small basket full of rice husk and emptied half of the content into the hearth. She then struck a matchstick and lighted a split piece of pinewood. With the help of the sooty pinewood flame she started a smoky fire in the small heap of rice husk. The heat produced by the rice husk fire dried the rain-soaked firewood. Slowly, the firewood started burning and leaped into flames. She placed an aluminium cooking vessel, outer surface of which was covered with a thick layer of black soot, over the fire and heaved a sigh of relief.

Plop . . . plop . . . plop.

Raindrops dripped off the ceiling after passing through the perforations in the old rusted corrugated iron sheet roof and fell directly into buckets, tubs and whatever vessels available in her house that she had strewn all over the room. In her ordeal of lighting a fire in the hearth she had forgotten the leaking roof. The sound of the steady trickle suddenly attracted her attention to the water collected in the vessels. All were now overflowing and flooding the already damp earthen floor. She hurriedly picked them up one by one and emptied the water outside. Outside, it was pitch-dark. After putting each of the vessels in their respective places, she started mopping the floor when she heard someone calling her from outside.

"Eche-Sakhi . . . Eche-Sakhi"

The voice seemed vaguely familiar but she could not immediately recognise it. She stopped what she was doing and paid her full attention to the voice.

The voice repeated, "Eche-Sakhi . . . Eche-Sakhi. Have you gone to bed so early?"

She could now place the voice. The caller was unmistakably Anou, one of her distant cousins.

"I'm still awake. I'm in the kitchen. The front door is not bolted. Just push it open and come inside."

Anou pushed the door open and came inside. Sakhi left mopping the floor unfinished. She brought a rickety stool and offered it to him to sit. To hide her embarrassment at the condition of her house she meekly said,

"It's so unexpected. You've come here for the first time. That too, at such an odd hour. What brought you here?"

Anou did not say anything. He looked around the room as he sat on the stool offered to him. The single room house with a leaking roof was not a place, which one could proudly call his or her home. A corner of the room served as the kitchen. He saw the two children; a girl aged about five and her younger brother, sitting silently on a cot in a corner of the room. They were watching him intently with their innocent eyes tense with hunger. He also noticed the baby on her back.

"So, you have three children. I have brought nothing for them."

"It's all right. All day long they did nothing except munching. They had just finished a packet of biscuits, the ever-hungry lots." She lied but inwardly she cursed her fate, the abject poverty—she had not been able to feed her children two square meals a day.

Tonu, her husband worked as a driver of a truck, which plied on the National Highways to transport consumer goods from Guwahati to Imphal, the capital city of the land-locked state of Manipur, located in the centre of a lovely valley surrounded by hills on all sides. He was orphaned at a young age. Except for a married elder sister, who stayed in a far-off village he had no close relative. On her side also, Shakhi had no well-to-do relative who could help and support her family. She was the eldest child of her parents, who lived hand to mouth. Her younger brothers were still in school.

It was very difficult to meet both the ends with her husband's meagre income. With her small children to look after, she could not leave the house to work to earn the much-needed money. However, she never remained idle. She grew vegetables around the house to meet her family's requirement. To supplement her husband's income she hand-knitted woollen clothes whenever she got orders. Torrents of the monsoon rain had spoiled her garden. The winter was still a long way off; no order for knitting was forthcoming. She counted over and over again every single paise of the money her husband gave her to run the family.

The prolonged road blockade had not only dwindled her husband's earning but had also made the price of essential commodities soar sky high. Some of the essential consumable items had simply vanished from the open market. Only those who could afford to pay exorbitant prices could still buy the items in black.

"I've just returned from Guwahati by bus. We reached here late by more than two hours because of the road blockade. We had to wait a long time for the police escort at a place just across the state border. There, I met Ebai-Tonu. He has been stranded at the place for the last two days. He is worried about you and the children"

"When is he reaching here?"

"No idea. More than fifty to sixty trucks are stranded there now. Police can escort only four or five trucks at a time. Passenger buses are given the priority."

"How long will this blockade last? Those mean and heartless people, how can they hold all the people of the state at ransom only to achieve their selfish goal!"

"God knows, when they'll lift the blockade! The chance of lifting the blockade in the near future is very remote."

Anou took out two hundred-rupee notes and gave them to Shakhi.

"Ebai-Tonu had given me the money to give it to you. That's why I've come here."

Sakhi's face brightened up. Still holding the currency notes in her hand, she said, "Thank you so much for taking all the troubles to come here to hand over the money. I'm sorry that I couldn't offer you even a cup of tea."

Anou got up and said, "It's quite late. My family must be worried about me. I must leave now." He left hurriedly.

Two days had passed after Anou's visit to her house. Dusk had fallen. Another day was coming to end. Tonu had not come yet. Sakhi's mind was restless. She was kneeling in front of the tulsi plant in the courtyard and lighting a cheap joss stick. Her two older children were also kneeling near her while the youngest one was on her back. She stuck the lighted joss stick in the damp ground and placed a burning lamp beside it. The live joss stick filled the air with a pleasant smell and sanctified the place. The family said their daily evening prayer together—an age-old tradition still kept alive in her household.

After saying her prayer, as Shakhi slowly opened her eyes she saw someone entering the gate and coming towards her. She stood up and waited for the newcomer to come nearer. When he was closer, she recognised him. He was Ebomcha, her husband's handyman, who always accompanied him wherever he went. Seeing him alone and the expression on his face alarmed her.

He called out in a shaky voice, "*Eteima.*" It seemed that he wanted to say something but words choked at his throat.

"Yes. What's it? Where's your *Tada?*"

Ebomcha stood silently without uttering a word. After a while he meekly said, "I've brought a very sad news. *Tada* met with an accident."

A sudden chill went up her spine.

"What? How badly injured is he?"

"*Tada* has left for the heavenly abode."

Suddenly she felt dizzy and everything around her started spinning like a top. Her legs could no longer support her weight. She slowly sat down on the ground. He continued to speak but she could no longer hear what he was saying.

"*Tada* was driving the truck and following a convoy. I was also in the truck. While taking a sharp turn on the road, some people hiding in the thick forests on the hillside started pelting stones. One of the stones found its target and smashed the windscreen of the truck. *Tada* was temporarily blinded. He lost the control of the truck. It went headlong down a deep gorge. That's all I can remember before I lost consciousness."

"When I opened my eyes I was lying on a bed in the District Hospital. The owner of the truck and some policemen were standing beside me. One of the policemen recorded my statement. Only after the completion of recording my statement, they informed me about *Tada*. He had been killed in the accident."

Shakhi was in a state of delirium—not listening to him but fighting hard to overcome her emotions. Ebomcha was not aware of that and went on with his story.

"I was discharged after first aid for a few minor scratches. They've sent me in a jeep to inform you. *Mahajan* has stayed behind to complete some formalities and claim *Tada*'s material remains after the post-mortem. They will be here any minute, now."

Shakhi embraced her two fatherless children who had been watching her silently. Her baby on her back also did not make any sound as if he knew the ordeal his mother was going through. She was not aware how long she and her children had remained like that. It was already very dark when she noticed Ebomcha still standing near her in the light thrown by the headlights of a jeep stopping near her gate.

After a while, one man with a bright lantern entered the gate followed by a group of people carrying a coffin covered with a white cloth. They placed the coffin on the ground near her without making the slightest noise. Someone from the group uncovered the face for her to see. In the light of the lantern, her husband's serene face, with eyes closed tight, was clearly visible.

It was her elder son, the second child, who broke the silence.

"*Ema,* why is *Baba* sleeping in the box?"

18

Fifty Years

Only fifteen days were left before she had to bid goodbye to the country of her dreams, a multi-lingual and multi-racial country with a rich cultural heritage—a great country where everyone is free to follow any faith of his or her choice, a country so vast that it enjoys every type of climate, from the hot tropical summer in the South to the jittery cold winter with heavy snowfall in the North. In the East, it enjoys the heaviest rainfall on the Earth. In the West, there lies a vast desert. Snow capped mountains guard its northern borders and open seas protect its southern borders. Its ancient philosophy can still satisfactorily answer the most difficult and critical present day question, be it on human relationship or science and technology.

She had come to visit the country not as a tourist but as a pilgrim with a purpose, to quench her thirst for a firsthand knowledge of her roots. She was proud that half of her roots belonged to the country. Her father hailed from the north-eastern part of the country—a small lovely valley surrounded by hills on all sides, whose natural beauty can be rivalled by only a few places on the surface of the Earth. It took her more than two years to gain entry into the secluded part of the country.

After several disappointing tries, her persuasion bore fruit at last, she got permission to enter the valley and stay there for three weeks.

Her parents were separated when she was barely three. All she knew about her father was that he had come to England to pursue advance studies in medicine. During his stay in London, he fell in love with her mother, a British and married her. About two years after the separation, they were divorced. Her mother married again and she moved in her stepfather's house with her. Before her mother's second marriage, her father used to visit her every weekend but after the marriage he completely stopped coming.

Her father, a keen lover of plants, had tried to grow many plants of different varieties in an unheated porch in the winter without much success. In the summer he did not find any problem but the winter was altogether a different story. After many unsuccessful attempts, one December he emptied a packet of seeds in a sink in the porch—he did not bother to sow the seeds properly. With his wife demanding more attention and the tight schedule at the hospital, where he worked, he had no time to spare. He had completely forgotten about the seeds. When spring had melted the snow, a new family member arrived. One fine morning after returning from the maternity home, the joyous couple went out to the porch holding their first child together in their arms, to bask the baby, a petite little girl in the mellow life-giving rays of the Sun, the baby's first ever contact with a celestial body after stepping into this world. Plants with colourful floral heads had fully covered the sink in the corner. The seeds had germinated and survived the fierce winter on their own, without any protection. Spring had renewed their vigour. To show their gratitude to the King of all seasons, they had sent up numerous floral heads, which gently opened in the warmth of the morning sun showing their smiling faces. On seeing the beautiful alpine flowers in her porch, the young mother exclaimed in admiration.

"Viola!"

The young father mistook her admiration of the flowers as calling the baby.

"Viola, a wonderful name for the baby!"

Little did they suspect that their little daughter would meet the same fate as the violas. When she turned seven, her mother and stepfather died in a car accident. Her father had already left the country and returned to his native place. Her mother was the only one who knew his whereabouts. After the funeral, she moved in her maternal uncle's house in the country. Viola grew up in the country and blossomed into a charming young woman, almost unaided like the alpine flower. After graduating from the country high school, she got a scholarship to advance her studies in London.

She was working on a study of the Raj when she decided to visit India, her father's country. Her study often took her to the British Museum, where she spent hours at a stretch in the reading room. One day in the summer, on her way to the British Museum she was about to go on the moving stairs going up to the Tottenham Court Road when she saw a group of people in the underground. The male members of the group were wearing *dhoti* and *kurta,* the Indian male attire. It was the strange dresses of the women in the group, which aroused her curiosity. They were wearing long horizontally striped skirt-like dress with embroidered borders. Fine clothes with beautiful woven floral-designs wrapped their bodies above the waist.

Viola sensed a very strange inexplicable feeling that she belonged to the group and she was one of them. She turned and slowly walked towards them as if she were drawn by an invisible but very powerful force. One guide-cum-interpreter was with the group. From him she learnt that they were a cultural troupe from Manipur, a remote place in the north-eastern corner of India. Among the group, there were dancers, musicians and singers.

She mused, "So, they are from Manipur, my father's place. It may be the reason of my strange feeling of closeness to them."

Through the interpreter, she spoke to one of the women. Her name was Ebemhal. She was a Manipuri Dance exponent and the leader of the dancers in the troupe. She invited Viola to witness their next performance. After noting the place and the timings of the performance, she parted from the group.

Viola watched the dance recital spellbound. The graceful movements and the intricate foot-steps had so enthralled her that she decided to learn Manipuri Dance. She met Ema-Ebemhal after the performance and told her about her intention to learn Manipuri Dance. She welcomed her intention and encouraged her but the problem was that she neither knew nor could suggest any place outside Manipur where she could learn Manipuri Dance. Her face lit up when Viola told her of her decision to come to Manipur. Viola left after collecting Ema-Ebemhal's home address.

With her decision to learn Manipuri Dance the picture was coming into shape like the pieces of a zig-saw puzzle falling into places—her work on the study of the Raj, her wish to trace her roots and her decision to learn Manipuri Dance seemed to fit in one place. She was disappointed when she learnt of the restrictions to the entry of foreigners into Manipur. She wrote to Ema-Ebemhal and obtained a paper sponsoring her to learn Manipuri Dance under her guidance, for which she would also arrange and be responsible for her stay at Imphal, the capital of Manipur. Armed with the sponsorship paper Viola applied for visa to enter Manipur and stay there. She got Indian visa for three months, all right. After that she had to apply separately for Protected Area Permit (PAP) to enter Manipur. With great difficulty she got PAP for three weeks.

She spent the three weeks at Ema-Ebemhal's house as a guest, picking up a few basic steps and collecting materials, which would enable her to practice alone back in London. Equipped with the sketchy information she knew about her father, she made inquiries but never disclosed her true identity for she wanted to surprise him. She learnt from a reliable source that her father had married again after his return from England and had two sons, her half-brothers, from the second marriage. He was said to be staying at a far off place in the hills. But with her preoccupation in learning Manipuri dance and restrictions to move about after dark, the time available at her disposal was too short to locate and meet him.

During her short stay, she mentally made a note of many unusual and strange things she noticed about the life of the people in Imphal, just the opposite of the image she had conceived since her childhood. "Unusually large numbers of armed security personnel, some of them in combat-dress, are deployed along the roads, reminding one of the great battles fought in the valley during the Second World War. People live in perpetual fear of some unseen forces. Except on compulsion they never stay out after dark but prefer to remain indoors. People are wary of strangers, especially teenagers. They will never speak to anyone until and unless they are very sure of his identity. It is a pity that they, who were once very strong, jovial, friendly and hospitable people, have now been reduced to meek and frightened people. To sum up, the present day Manipuri Society is very sick; some mysterious evil disease is eating into them."

She once got a chance to move outside Imphal and go for sightseeing. She went to Sendra, an islet in the Loktak, a large fresh water lake, connected to the mainland by road built on earthen embankment. Standing at the highest point there, she got a good view of the lake and the valley surrounded by ranges of hills. She gasped at the breathtaking scene that lay before her, a rare sight that would remain imprinted in her memory forever—the floating huts of fishermen built on *phumdi* (mat of humus floating on water) anchored with long poles of bamboo, the deep blue hills in the distance and the white fluffy-cloud-decorated blue sky mirrored on the vast expanse of water surface, dugout canoes cutting across spreading ripples on the calm surface!

Asish, a Delhi based photographer, was already there when she reached Sendra. He had come to this remote corner of India to capture the images of places not frequented by many people. He was on the lookout of a model, an uncommon face, for a series of photographs, which a renowned textile house was planning to release to commemorate the 50th Year of India's Independence. He got a special contract to do the photographs with the approval of the Board of Directors. He was also given a free hand to select a model of his choice and the locations to shoot the photographs. He wanted to prove his worth and bring out a lifetime best series of photographs. The moment he saw Viola, he was sure that he had found the face, which could launch his career to new heights. Viola's face showed the features of her mixed parentage—a round face with small sparkling deep-blue eyes, a slightly upturned but not very sharp nose, high cheek bones, a small hollow in the left cheek suggesting a faint dimple, a sensuous mouth with full lips and a pointed chin. To sum up her face could be best described as "A Caucasoid Face with domineering Oriental Features." Her face radiated warmth and friendliness all around.

She was still deeply absorbed in the marvels of Nature's display before her when Asish approached her with a request to take a few pictures of her with his camera. He handed her his visiting card.

She glanced at the card and she blurted out excitedly, "Oh my! So nice to meet you." After a brief pause, she continued, "I'm Viola T. Fraser from London. I have come to Manipur to learn Manipuri Dance. I have never had my photograph taken by a professional, before."

The Sun played hide-and-seek with the white fluffy clouds. When the Sun hid behind the clouds, Asish saw his chance and took two shots of Viola in the revealing light, one close-up and the other full. Once he saw her through the lens, his visual perception at the first sight was confirmed. "Photographs do not lie but it can manipulate the images—it can highlight the plus points and hide the unwanted parts. It can make a dull face look lively and attractive but it can never change the subject altogether. It cannot create an unusual and uncommon face out of the ordinary common face. Viola's face has all the features and plus-points of a rare exceptional beauty that will capture a photographer's imagination and make him wild with ecstasy—her face, a raw uncut diamond, which can be transformed into a magnificent invaluable gem in the hands of an expert gem-cutter."

He told her of his plans to take a series of photographs in three different sessions covering three aspects of Indian life, to commemorate India's Fifty Years of self-rule. Photographs in the first session would be shot in a studio, the second in palaces and forts all over the country and the third in the locale of a remote village. He had chalked out the details of his plan immaculately but he had a problem—the problem of finding the right face to model his dreams. He was careful not to mention what he thought of her.

He cautiously said, "If you are interested, you can be the model."

"It sounds interesting but I have no idea of modelling."

He was delighted that she had not flatly refused his offer. He knew that she would give in if he made the offer more appealing.

"There is a first time for everything. Posing for photographs is not difficult at all. You just stand in front of the camera and be your natural self, leave the rest to me."

"I'm sorry I don't think I can make it. I've one more week to stay in Manipur. After that, there'll be only two months left before my visa expires. I want to make the best use of the time available with me, to see more of India before I leave."

"I have a suggestion. We can combine the photo-sessions and your sightseeing tours. The photo-sessions will cover palaces and forts, reminiscence of the Raj. Some of the shots will be taken at a remote village. If you accept to model for the photographs, you can see many important places of India, which you would otherwise miss. I will make all the arrangements and bear the expenses of your travel and stay."

She was not very keen on modelling but the very mention of 'the Raj' suddenly aroused her interest. "Please give me some time to think over it."

"OK, I can wait till you finish your dance lessons here. I'll be leaving for Delhi, tomorrow. You can ring me up at the number given in my card."

She had been cornered. She found it virtually impossible to refuse the tempting offer but she simply said, "I'll let you know."

"Take your own time but I expect a positive answer. When you call me, you can name your price. As a professional, I want to settle everything beforehand so that we don't land into trouble later."

After two days, Asish was in his studio. He had enlarged the two photographs of Viola, which he had taken. He held the close-up shot closely and then hung it on a line with clips. He moved back a little and looked at it from a distance. He was sure that her face was the most attractive and charming face he had photographed if not the most beautiful—a unique face. She would stand out perfectly among the hundreds of models he knew. Strangely, her face closely resembled the typical face of a Manipuri woman, a Mongoloid face with traces of Caucasoid features, which he had seen at the women's market in Imphal. He brushed aside the thought, "It may be my imagination or just the coincidence that I have taken Viola's photograph in Manipur." He was admiring her photograph when he received her call. She had accepted to model for the photographs.

The terms and conditions of modelling for the photographs were settled. It was planned that after leaving Manipur, she would come to Delhi by a direct flight. He would receive her at the airport and arrange for her accommodation. The photographs of the first session would be shot at his studio in Delhi. Then they would proceed for the next session covering important places associated with the Raj. Photographs would be taken in the morning and at sunset. At other times, she would be free to roam around for sightseeing. She would model free of cost if he agreed to bear the expenses of her travel and accommodation. The last session would take one whole day at a remote village. Before leaving India, he would show her the prints and give her one copy of each of the shots. She would formally approve the selected photographs before releasing them to the press.

In the studio, Asish was assisted by a dress designer, a coiffeur, a beautician and a lighting assistant. Viola faced the camera and experienced for the first time how she could transform into different persons. She posed wearing the latest styles—a loose-fitting stripped trouser-suit, an exquisite lemon-yellow embroidered gown, a plunging décolleté dress with floral prints and a matching scarf. She had never imagined how a masculine dress like a trouser-suit could look so feminine under the right conditions. The artificial lights thrown from front, side and back created a dramatic effect. For one particular shot she was made to stand before a bright source of light and face the camera to create a "halo" effect. The first session took two days to complete.

For the second session, Viola travelled all over the country with Asish and his assistant. During this session she got opportunity to see palaces and forts connected with the Raj. She posed for the photographs in period costumes—flowing gowns, which emphasised her slender waist and revealed the contours of her upper body, crochet scarves, fancy hats decorated with coloured feathers, white gloves, matching clothe-purses and colourful umbrellas. Vintage cars, Standard Coventry Tourer with carbide gas lights and Darracq Tourer with rear wheel brakes, both 1913 models were hired to create lifelike scenes of the bygone days. Some of the shots were taken in revealing light with the cars in the foreground and a magnificent palace in the background. The second session lasted more than a month.

The last session was yet to be completed but only fifteen days were left before she had to leave the country. She was excited that she would be going to a remote village where no outsider had ever trodden before, for the final session. Another reason of her excitement was that she had been given the chance to pick and choose local dresses and ornaments for the photographs, herself at a market on the way to the village.

She pondered, "So long I have seen only the illusive side of India. The heart of India lies in the rural life. Now, I will be able to see the pure unspoilt India of my dreams, which has not been influenced and corrupted by the modern materialistic world."

On the appointed day she got up very early and took a refreshing shower with cold water, a habit, which she had picked up and thoroughly enjoyed, after coming to India. She had fresh orange juice, corn salad with boiled carrot and a slice of bread for breakfast. The Sun was just above the horizon when they started off for their destination in two hired jeeps. She, Asish and a driver occupied one jeep while the other jeep was occupied by Asish's assistant, a woman helper and another driver. After driving for about an hour they came to a market and stopped there.

Asish sent the other jeep to their destination as an advance party while he and Viola got down and roamed around the market. The traders had just started opening their stalls and arranging the display of their wares. To her, the place seemed like a scene from the Arabian Nights. She surveyed all the stalls before making her selection. Asish helped her to choose colourful *ghagras* and *cholis* with appliqué-works. She also picked *chudders* with tie and dye works, glass bangles and silver ornaments.

After leaving the market, they followed an uneven and dusty track to their destination. They passed clusters of mud plastered huts with terracotta tile roofs. A group of village belles with earthen pots balanced on their heads, their faces partially covered with *ghoongat*, giggled as they passed them. The jeep stopped at the foot of a hillock, under the shade of a majestic peepul tree. Asish's assistant had already pitched a tent, where Viola would be able to change her clothes and apply make-up in privacy.

A little way off some women were busy at the community well collecting water in earthen pots. Asish got down. He went to the well and talked to the women. All of them turned their faces and laughed heartily when they saw Viola. He requested them to remain there for a while so that they could be photographed with Viola—their presence would make the picture look more authentic and natural.

They refused to be photographed. Superstitious folks, they believed that their life would be shortened if their images were extracted into photographs. The woman helper helped Viola to change into a *ghagra* and a matching *choli*. She then adorned herself with the glass bangles and the silver ornaments. She did not apply any make-up except a large round vermilion *bindi* on her forehead. She posed near the well and the first shot of the day was taken. Asish used a colour correcting filter and imaginatively exploited the powerful sunlight creating strong contrast between light and shadow, to emphasise the impression of tropical India.

In the afternoon, they took a break for lunch, which Asish had brought in the jeep. The last shot of the day, which was also the last shot of the session, was taken on the top of the hillock with Viola facing the camera and the setting Sun as the source of back light. When they started off for the return journey after packing their things, it was already dark. Viola and Asish sat in the front jeep. The other jeep followed them closely. Except for the jeeps' headlights the whole place was engulfed in total darkness. The place that was humming with people during the day had been transformed into a phantasmal land. The drive was very rough with the jeep negotiating holes and ditches all along the narrow dusty track. In her eagerness to see the rural life of India, she had not felt the uncomfortable drive while coming. With darkness creeping in from all sides, she now felt a strange sense of suffocation as if she were inhaling black soot with every breath she took. When they neared a village, she saw a dim lamp burning in the courtyard of a house and felt better.

The jeep slipped into a ditch and both the right side wheels got stuck between two smooth and slippery boulders. Asish and the occupants of the other jeep pushed hard while the driver was at the wheels with the engine at full throttle but could not move the jeep. It was impossible to free the jeep without removing one of the boulders. They needed help of the villagers. Asish went to the house where a lamp was burning in the courtyard. Viola followed him. The head of the family, an old man was in the courtyard, sitting on a *charpoy* with a small hookah in his hand. When he saw Asish entering the gate with Viola closely following him, he called out loudly to his family members, "*Koi hai? Dekho kaun aya?*" (Is anyone there? See who has come?)

A bare-chested man with thick brows and a big moustache, wearing a turban on his head, carrying a kerosene lamp in one hand and a long stick in the other, came out of the house. Asish went ahead and spoke to him while Viola remained near the gate. The man went inside the house and soon came out followed by a woman, whose head was covered with the loose end of her *sari*.

All three of them, Asish, the bare-chested man and his wife came toward the gate where Viola was standing. The man put down the stick and the lamp. Then both the husband and wife greeted Viola with folded hands. She returned the greeting with folded hands. Asish explained that he would be going with the man to the neighbouring houses to ask for help to remove the boulders. They wanted her to wait at the house till they came back. They soon left after that.

The wife motioned Viola to follow her and sit on an unoccupied *churpoy* next to the one where the old man, her father-in-law was sitting. She said something to him. He immediately stood up and said something while greeting Viola with folded hands. The only words she could make out of what he said, were '*Vilayati Memsahib*'. She returned the greeting and sat down. The woman went inside the house and soon came out carrying a brass tumbler with water, which she offered to Viola. Not knowing what to do she took the tumbler and hold it in her hand for a long time. She took a sip and put the tumbler on the floor. It tested like brine. She guessed, "Untreated water from tube well." The woman covered her mouth and giggled nervously. She then went inside the house.

From where she was sitting, Viola could see the woman through the open door. She was cooking something on a smoky *chula.* Putrid smell of dried cow-dung being burnt lingered around the whole place. After a while she came out and spoke to her father-in-law politely. He said something to her in a commanding tone. She went in and came out after a while, carrying two brass *thalis.* One, she gave to her father-in-law and the other to Viola. Viola took the *thali* and looked at the contents—one big dry *roti,* a slice of onion, one big green chilli and a pinch of salt. She mused, "So, this is what people in the villages eat for supper."

When Asish returned with the bare-chested man to call her after pulling out the jeep from the ditch, the *thali* was still in her hand, with everything intact. She left without touching the food at all. She felt sorry that she had not reciprocated the hospitality of the simple village folks. She spent the remaining few days before her departure, roaming around the countryside and the slums in the cities. She saw more of the life in the villages, which confirmed her first experience. The half-starved, oppressed and illiterate villagers led a miserable life miles apart from the glittering world of the affluent, educated and westernised people living in the cities. Before her departure she received copies of all the photographs, which Asish had taken. All were masterpieces. She approved the few selected ones for releasing to the press.

The day of her departure had arrived. She reported at the airport and boarded the plane that would take her back to England. The aircraft started moving slowly and taxied to the runway for takeoff. She was disappointed. Her mission of meeting her father was unaccomplished and the image of India, the country of her dreams, where half of roots belonged, had also been shattered. She took one last look of the country of her dreams through the window and closed her eyes. The gloomy faces of the helpless people of Manipur, oppressed by an unseen force and the shy and docile faces of the starved and deprived people of the village pleading for mercy, flashed before her one by one.

"O my India! A mysterious country! Fifty long years of self rule, majority of the people still live in the dark ages!"

Glossary of Manipuri words

Abok Macha—small granny (*Abok:* Granny; *Macha:* Small)

Baba—father

Bora—a preparation of pea-flour and shredded vegetables deeply fried in oil.

Bora-yonbis—*bora*-sellers

Boroi Heingan—jujube jam

Cheche—elder sister

Dona—banana-leaf-cup

Ebai—brother-in-law

Eche—elder sister

Ema—mother

Enaphi—Manipuri woman's garment; a length of cloth used for wrapping the upper portion of the body.

Ene—Aunt (*Ene*-Binashakhi or Aunt-Binashakhi)

Eteima—sister-in-law

Ganja—marijuana

Khudei—a piece of cotton cloth, folded and carried on the shoulder by aged men; also worn like *dhoti* by man

Lairik-taba—religious discourse usually held at temples in the afternoon

Lanmei Thanbi—will-o'-the-wisp (a natural phenomena; a mysterious light seen at night flickering over marshes) *"Lanmei Thanbi toi toi. Hangen poura kit"* Roughly translated it means, "Come *Lanmei Thanbi*, come, if you dare. We'll nab you with *hangen* (bamboo skeleton used for stretching Chinese fishing nets) and *poura* (bamboo pole on which *hangen* is attached or tied)."

Meira Paibi—social organisation of women formed to fight against social evils and atrocities committed by armed personnel.

Paba—father

Pheijom—dhoti, Indian male attire

Phige phanek—silk garment of a woman covering the lower portion of the body

Phumdi—floating humus matter

Tada—Elder brother

Yama-Doot (Sanskrit origin)—Envoy of Yama, the Hindu god of death